I0725048

# DON'T BREAK MY HEART

*A Psychological Thriller*

## GERTIE GREYSON

Copyright © 2025 by Gertie Greyson

All rights reserved.

Without in any way limiting the author's exclusive rights under copyright, any use of this publication to "train" generative artificial intelligence (AI) technologies to generate text is expressly prohibited. The author reserves all rights to license uses of this work for generative AI training and development of machine learning language models.

This is a work of fiction, created without use of AI technology. Any names, characters, places or incidents are products of the author's imagination and used in a fictitious manner. Any resemblance to actual people, places, or events is purely coincidental or fiction.

All rights reserved, including the right to reproduce this book or portions thereof in any form whatsoever.

First Edition: November 11, 2025
Ebook ISBN: 978-1-950141-93-7

# DESCRIPTION

In the quiet town of Rosebud Grove, everyone adores Nicole Kelly. Brilliant, compassionate, and engaged to the hospital's chief of medicine, she's the kind of nurse patients trust. When a health crisis threatens her life, the entire town rallies as Nicole undergoes a miraculous heart transplant. She survives, but survival comes at a price.

Almost immediately, Nicole senses something is different. The sudden flashes of anger, the strange impulses, the haunting nightmares—none of it feels like her. Then come the discoveries: other organ recipients meeting untimely ends and a donor whose past may not have been as clean as the gift he left behind. And when a desperate young woman collapses on Nicole's doorstep with a chilling warning, Nicole is thrust into a deadly game she can't escape.

As secrets unravel, Nicole finds herself torn between her reputation as Rosebud Grove's golden girl and the darkness that lures her in. Friends become suspects, allies turn into threats, and the line between sanity and madness blurs. With bodies piling up and danger closing in, Nicole must confront the truth about her legacy—before it's snatched away from her.

***Don't Break My Heart*** *is a haunting domestic thriller set in the misty redwoods of Northern California, where small-town perfection hides unspeakable secrets and even the most beloved heroes can harbor terrifying darkness.*

# PROLOGUE

exas

THE DAY DAWNS with electricity in the air. I can feel the change the second the garish overhead lights flip on and wake up the cell block. Voices down the hall echo off the walls as my heart begins to pound. The drab off-white ceiling with the water stain in the corner is the same one I've woken up to for fifteen years. I reckon it'll be the same for the next fifteen years too, though I won't be around to confirm that suspicion.

"Bixler!" a voice barks from nearby.

I roll on the lumpy mat they call a mattress for the last time and face the doorway. My least favorite prison guard eyes me through the bars like I'm the dog shit beneath his boot. He wrinkles his lip in a snarl I've become all too familiar with.

"They want you showered and presentable." Officer Truett's words are clipped, like he hates that he has to offer me something as enjoyable as a cold shower in a communal bathroom with mold growing between the tiles.

I sit up, placing my bare feet on the concrete. I feel younger than I have in a long time. That same rush of energy I felt before I took a life is racing through my veins. I haven't felt it in so long I wondered if it had left me for good. I shoot Officer Truett a smile. The one that made all the women trust me way back when. His answering snarl just feeds my glee.

Today is the day.

I smile all through my supervised shower. I smile as fellow prisoners give me a wide berth like every other day. You see, the spirit to kill, to snuff out a life and take perverse pleasure in seeing the light dim in their eyes, is not something you lose, even if you're sentenced to a life behind bars. It festers actually. The urge to kill becomes so unbearable, so out of reach, one might resort to killing hardened inmates with one's bare hands just to know one still can. Reputations are everything in here, and mine is as pristine as a blanket of fresh snow on Christmas morning.

*Once a killer, always a killer*, is what Officer Truett spat at me after another prisoner thought he'd try his luck and quickly found that an animal lived behind this human facade. The ol' guard ain't wrong. In fact, I'm counting on his belief holding true.

"Meal's in your cell," Officer Truett grunts as I come out of the shower in a fresh pair of trousers and button-down shirt. I slide a hand through my wet hair, tousling the curling strands that I attempted to tame with gel, turning my dark hair even darker. Another benefit of today being my last day: they give you gel and a comb so you can look presentable when you meet your maker.

"Could have used these fancy clothes when I met the priest yesterday," I mutter back, walking in front of him back to my cell.

"Pretty sure God is bothered by worse things than your outfit, Bixler."

My lips lift on one side. That might be the first joke Officer Truett has ever cracked in my presence. Breakfast is a heaping plate of scrambled eggs—the real ones, not the powder they mix with too much water—bacon, waffles, French fries, and a full carafe of black coffee. I partake of my favorite meal with gusto, not a care in the world.

Today is the day.

I've barely washed it all down with the scalding coffee when Officer Truett is back, his bulk blocking the light coming from the single yellow bulb in the hallway.

"Missed me already, Truett?"

"Get up," he snaps.

I brush crumbs off my shirt and stand as if I have all the time in the world. I know it pisses him off. Short of killing him, it gives me great pleasure to make him angry. I know it frustrates him not to be able to kill me too. A killer always recognizes another killer, and I see it in ol' Officer Truett.

"Time for my IV treatment?" I ask casually, as if I'm headed for a day at the health spa.

Perhaps I'm not the normal prisoner on death row facing the inevitable end in a sterile room with looks of disgust and relief from onlookers that I will finally take my last waste-of-a-human breath. Because I know something they don't. I've taken multiple precautions that ensure that this is not the end of Cyrus Gene Bixler. For all the lives I've taken, I have saved more.

His eyes narrow while he unlocks and holds the door open for me. "Just walk."

He's a man of few words, which I can respect. I, too, spoke few words when I was working. I didn't want conversation with my victims. I wanted that *feeling*. The rush of blood that raced through my veins and made me feel superhuman. I needed my heart to pump at twice its normal speed, telling me that I was truly living. It was always an exchange of energy. As theirs faded, mine increased.

There's no fanfare as I walk the hallway for the last time, hands bound in front of me. Nothing to mark this walk as anything different than the thousands of times before. Some of my fellow inmates give a head nod of acknowledgement. Most don't bother to look up.

Officer Truett walks slower than normal, as if I may need to savor these last few moments. But as I discussed with the priest yesterday, I don't have regrets. I don't have doubts. I'm ready to enter the next stage of my life. Looking forward to it, actually. I always wondered what my victims felt like as their life drained away. Now I'll know. It'll make every killing that much more complete. That much more intimate.

The room that awaits me is sterile, the gray flooring matching the gray walls and the gray ceiling. The lights from above cast a garish yellow glow on the gray metal gurney. Brown leather straps hooked to the gurney break up the monotony of the room. Officer Truett gestures for me to climb on the gurney, which I do, sitting and staring directly at the window across from me. I can't see who might be on the other side of the pane of glass, but I can imagine. I can see the faces of every life I took stamped across the features of their loved ones, here to fulfill some sort of deranged thirst for revenge.

My dying here today won't bring their loved ones back.

Expelling my last breath won't undo the years of heartache.

My impact on this earth will continue, even when I don't.

Redemption is mine and no one can take that from me.

Which is why I'm grinning as the doctor enters the room and Officer Truett straps me to the table with cold efficiency.

"Today's the day," Truett says finally, as if I didn't know.

He nods, confirming to himself, then steps back, leaving my side for the last time.

The doctor's surgical mask hides most of his expression but the eyes are enough. He feels nothing as he begins his monotone explanation of events. This is just a job for him. As soon as he's done with me, he'll go home to a wife and kids and a life where one less asshole like me is waiting in the shadows to steal it all away.

"Once you're sedated, we'll intubate and you'll essentially be on life support. Machines will take over your bodily function. The viewing will be over and we'll take you straight to the operating room. Do you understand?"

I nod that I do.

The doctor hesitates for just a moment. A flicker of emotion seeps into his dark eyes. "Enjoy hell," he mutters so quietly that no one could possibly have heard him except me.

My grin flares to life again, my heart pounding. "I'll see you there. Your killing is not so different than mine. Which keeps you up at night, doesn't it?"

His hands tremble ever so slightly as they make quick work of the job. The bite of the needle entering my arm is minimal. Humans aren't so hard to figure out. We all have wants and needs and fears. We have all done bad things right alongside the good. Who's to say which of us go to hell and which escape? No one is either all bad or all good, something even the priest reluctantly agreed with me on.

The beep of my heart rate fills the room. It quickens as my last seconds tick away. Warmth floods my body, sound quickly fades, and my body floats, hovering there in a peaceful rocking. A suspended hammock in time.

Today is the day...the killing continues.

I just never thought it would be me.

# CHAPTER ONE



"*L*et's walk in slowly, darling," Asher murmurs, placing a gentle kiss on my cheek that makes my battered heart speed up just from his presence.

I lift my nose in the air, a playfully defiant smile in place. His parents, Daniel and Josephine Kingsley, will be at one of those round banquet tables, judging every single detail of the woman attached to their son. Most likely finding my dress lacking, or my heels too low, or my lipstick just a shade too bright. Hundreds of pictures will be taken tonight to splash online and grace the front page of the *Grove Daily Times*. This is the hospital's largest fundraiser of the year, after all.

"Absolutely not. I feel fantastic. In fact, let's run inside when they announce your name."

Asher gives me one of his lopsided grins, the one that sent my heart flying through the clouds the first day I met him on the surgical floor of the hospital we both work at. Well, the hospital I used to work at. Asher is now chief of medicine, following in his father's footsteps, while I'm on medical leave. The ticking time bomb in my chest has finally neared its end.

He opens his mouth to say something that will surely be

both witty and endearing, but the doors to the ballroom fling open, cutting him off. The bright lights of the stage already find us.

"Please welcome our chief of medicine, Asher Kingsley!"

He's not God, but he may as well be here in the town of Rosebud Grove. The biggest, most innovative wing of the prestigious Rosebud Memorial Hospital is named the Kingsley Foundation, after his family.

And their incredible monetary donation.

We step forward, and as promised, Asher moves slowly, allowing me to cling to his arm as we walk through the crowd. People are on their feet in applause. Rich ones in tuxedos, influential ones dripping equally in diamonds and power, and the invisible ones who support them, going unnoticed by most. But I see them. I was one of them until Asher Kingsley took notice of a lowly resident over five years ago.

Red roses and thick dark greenery make every round table burst with color. Chandeliers overhead dance light strobes over the crowd. This ballroom is stunning, just like Josephine so meticulously planned. Next year, when I'm Mrs. Asher Kingsley, maybe I'll be the one coordinating this event.

Dear friends and coworkers reach out to hold my hand as we pass. Their smiles and encouragement are exactly what I need to hold my head high. Most of this community is comprised of good people trying to help society. Sometimes I get bogged down in the politics that come with being the chief of medicine's fiancée, but I always try to remember that people are inherently good.

With another kiss on my cheek and a gentle push into a chair next to his parents, Asher leaves my side and bounds up onto the stage to give the speech he rehearsed this morning as he shaved. He never looks nervous, just damn confident in his ability to have everyone here opening up their wallets and donating to the night's cause.

"And that, ladies and gentlemen, is why we need to continue our efforts in providing the highest quality medical care the West Coast has ever experienced. Under my watch and with your help, Rosebud Memorial will be synonymous with cutting edge innovation and elite healthcare."

Asher ends his speech with his trademark grin, looking both confidently debonair and next-door charming. It's a potent combination that works to keep the shareholders, donors, nurses, and patients happy. Asher can do no wrong in Rosebud Grove.

"Shoulders back," Josephine hisses in my ear.

I snap to attention, rolling them so far back my spine aches, I continue to clap enthusiastically, but demurely, for my fiancé as he makes his way offstage to shake hands. No one is watching me, but appearances must be kept up. Josephine has made sure I'm at the top of my game, even if I'm days away from my deathbed. No future daughter-in-law of hers will be caught slouching. I have to choke back a laugh at what she'd say if I'd shown up at the ballroom with my trusty oxygen tank in tow.

The swarm of people move closer to our table as Asher tries to make his way back. In unison, we stand, still clapping as Asher's golden head appears to my left. And then he's there, breaking through the crush of people and stretching his arms out to me.

"There's my love," he says loudly, walking past several outstretched arms to take me in his. I rest my cheek on his chest for the briefest of moments, wishing we were at home in our pajamas, settling in to watch a late-night documentary together.

"She's quite the belle of the ball, Asher," some kind gentleman says to my right.

I lift my head to see the gentleman's ruddy cheeks approach my fiancé. Asher lets me go to shake his hand. I can feel Josephine's scowl burning a hole on the side of my face. Even after four years of dating and almost a whole year of being engaged, she has not taken a liking to me. Despite Asher's attempts to find common ground between us, and my near constant cow-towing, Josephine has decided to hate me. Daniel, Asher's father, has decided I don't exist. I can count on one hand the number of times he's spoken directly to me. Never thought I'd appreciate being invisible, but the last thing I need is Daniel actively hating me too.

Asher pulls me into the circle of people, his arm like a steel band around my waist as he schmoozes with the crowd. "I couldn't do half of what I do without Nicole."

His praise flows over me, soothing all the scowl burns from his mother. For as uncertain is my future due to my failing heart, I am never uncertain about Asher's love. He is nothing short of my savior. He gives me an abundance of hope when my deteriorating condition gives me very little. He's proven that love does exist and it's just as exhilarating as all the Disney princess movies I watched growing up.

"How's the golden couple holding up?"

A warm presence covers my free side. I turn to see Ruby scanning the crowd around us with a fake smile plastered across her beautiful face. Her black dress sparkles in the lights from the overhead chandeliers, highlighting her enviable figure. Ruby Evans is beautiful, inside and out.

She and I became fast friends years ago, both of us brand-new nurses at Rosebud Memorial, full of false hope and idealized methods of taking care of patients. Tonight, she tosses a glance my way, shooting me a covert wink.

I look to Asher, the way he's handling the crowd with ease, a smile and handshake for everyone, staying long enough to make each person feel special. It's both a gift and a skill he's honed through years of training under his father's watchful eye.

"I'd say one half is good," I whisper back.

Ruby scans me from head to toe in a matter of a millisecond, her nurse's brain spinning. "Would you mind if I steal your fiancée away for a trip to the ladies'?" Ruby interrupts Asher's latest admirer.

Asher kisses me on the cheek and I'm released from the throng instantly. Ruby threads my hand through her elbow and pushes our way out the back of the ballroom. She's careful to move slowly, which I appreciate since I can't seem to catch my breath. It's ridiculous to be in my twenties, supposedly in the best shape of one's life, and I can't even walk across a ballroom without risk of passing out.

The ballroom door closes behind us and suddenly the loudest noise is no longer the music or the people, but the sound of my wheezing breath.

"I have the oxygen tank set up over here. No one will see us." She pushes a large palm frond out of the way to reveal a hidden alcove. As promised, my tank is set up next to a small love seat. I sink into it gratefully, pulling the cannula into my nose, leaning my head back with my eyes closed, and trying to breathe deeply. The couch cushions sink next to me.

"You shouldn't push yourself like this, Nic." Ruby's voice is kind but reproachful. She's the only one who still talks to me like I'm a regular girl. It's one of the things I love about her the most. Just maybe not right now.

I pry one eye open, already feeling more like myself. "Asher's mother would have been the one with a heart attack if I didn't show up to support him."

Ruby's scowl could compete with Josephine's. "Your heart is failing, Nic. I'm pretty sure that's a valid reason to skip a gala. At the very least, you should be wearing your oxygen."

"It doesn't go with my outfit," I deadpan.

Ruby doesn't laugh. I don't expect her to. We've had this discussion many times before. As a nurse, I know my oxygen saturation getting down into the seventies is a serious problem, but tell that to the Kingsleys. To wear my oxygen would be to show weakness. They were scandalized enough that Asher asked a woman with a heart condition to marry him. When I had to go on the transplant list last year, his parents planned an intervention, designed to get him to break up with me. Instead, he asked me to marry him.

Just one more reason I love Asher.

"If you keep this up, you won't make it to the altar," she says quietly, tears fogging up her pretty blue eyes. I reach over and squeeze her hand.

"I know. Which is why Asher and I decided to postpone until I get my new heart. I want to start a life with him knowing I won't be leaving him immediately."

Ruby grips me tighter. "He agreed?"

I nod. "I didn't give him much choice. His parents do have a bit of a point. Asking a dying girl to marry you is a bit crazy."

"You're not dying, Nicole," Ruby snaps, entirely too loudly.

I glance around, but don't see that anyone has caught us in our hiding place. "I have no intention of dying, I promise you that. I want to marry Asher and have his babies and live happily ever after. I also want to come back to work. Even if it's just a couple of days a week. Dying kind of puts a damper on all that."

Ruby lifts an eyebrow, a curve to her painted lips. "With your last name being Kingsley, you'll never have to work a day in your life again, girl."

I let go of her hand and lean my head back against the couch. Sometimes I wonder how I got here. How a poor girl with a single parent made it to the pinnacle of society in the Grove. How did I go from counting my pennies every paycheck to keeping track of which ball gown I wore to which event?

"Nicole?"

My head snaps up at the sound of Asher's voice. He sounds panicked and that has my abused heart speeding up. I rip the canula from my nose and stand. The room sways, but Ruby holds me up with her arm around my waist.

"Over here, Asher," she calls.

A moment later the palm frond moves and there he is, a Greek god in a tuxedo standing in our midst. A weird look is spreading across his face as his eyes land on me.

"Asher? Is everything okay?"

He doesn't stop to shove the canula back in my nose, or ask what my stats are like he does at least twenty times per day. He roughly pulls me into his arms and gazes down into my face with a look of awe. Or terror.

"Asher?" He's scaring me now. In all my nightmares of the future, my own demise was the one I imagined. Never his. Fear floods my chest as possibilities stream through my brain, each more horrifying. "What is it?"

"They have a heart for you."

A simple sentence. One I wasn't sure I'd ever hear.

"W-what?" I stutter.

Ruby hovers by me, never a third wheel but simply another leg on the stool that holds up this precarious life of mine.

Asher's face splits into a grin like nothing I've seen before. "A hospital I'm not familiar with called. They have a heart for you. Everything matches."

I blink. Ruby squeals. And then Asher is swooping me up into his arms, my heavy velvet dress not a deterrent at all.

"Let's go home and pack. If all goes well, surgery will be first thing tomorrow. They've agreed to let me scrub in."

"Oh my God," Ruby murmurs. Then she's hugging me,

pushing us both out of the alcove, her volume rising. "Go! I'll meet you at the house and pack her bag. You get her fed and hydrated."

Asher nods and strides out of the alcove, oblivious to the stares of everyone in the hallway outside the ballroom. I cling to his neck and try to assimilate the knowledge that I am getting everything I've ever wanted.

A new heart.

My soon-to-be husband.

The rest of my life.

It's mayhem as Asher begins to shout instructions at people around us. Word has spread that a heart is available. Someone rushes over with my purse. Another opens the door to the outside. The black limo we rented to go to the event screeches to the curb. The driver barely gets the door open before Asher is placing me gently inside.

"Congratulations, ma'am," our driver says with a tip of his hat.

Asher stands back up, raises his face to the moon, and lets out a whoop at the top of his lungs. Cheers from the stragglers around us have me giggling, tears stinging my eyes. I'm in shock. I'm elated.

I'm also scared.

Heart transplant surgery is a big operation. It's tricky. It's long. It's always rife with complications. If I make it off the table, the recovery will be long and painful and full of setbacks.

But for a shot at a life with Asher, I'll do it.

Asher closes my door. I see his mother catch his elbow before he runs over to the other side to get in. She whispers something in his ear that has his back straightening. He scowls down at her, but eventually nods his head. And then he's in the car, shouting instructions at the driver. He turns to me and takes my ice-cold hands in his.

"This is it, darling."

His eyes are so full of hope and love that I melt into the seat.

"But...how?" We both know the list is long and the wait is even longer. I figured I had at least another year before I got the call.

Asher smiles at me, rubbing my hands in his. "What did I tell you about the Kingsley luck? When you're with me, the whole world lies at your feet."

I exhale a lungful of air, the steady thrum of my heartbeat now a chant of hope instead of doom. I could question it further, but why? Far better to turn my brain to preparing for tomorrow. "I love you, you know."

Asher leans down and plucks a kiss from my lips. "And I love you, Nicole Kelly. Let's get you a new heart and then we can grow old together."

"You promise?" I look up at him like a child would her hero.

"I promise."

# CHAPTER TWO

"I've got to go get scrubbed in, darling. Are you ready?"

Asher hovers over my hospital bed, looking hot has hell in his navy-blue scrubs, not a trace of tiredness on his handsome face. I, on the other hand, look like an eighteenth-century ghost, ready to faint behind the drab hospital gown they changed me into before the sun had even come up. Once I'm recovered from this surgery, maybe I should petition Asher to do a fundraiser for nicer hospital gowns.

"I'm ready." I smile up at him, suddenly overcome with the sense that everything's about to change. That I could either die or be given new life on that operating table and there's no one I'd rather see before I take that leap than Asher. Tears fill my bloodshot eyes yet again. When I wasn't sleeping last night, brain whirling with all the possibilities, I was tearing up with gratitude. I'm an emotional basket case, hanging on by a thread.

Asher sees the tears and leans back down, pressing his forehead to mine, gazes locked. "I love you more than life itself. I will not let a single thing harm you in there, I promise you. We have a long life together ahead of us."

My throat closes up and all I can do is grip his forearm and nod, tears now leaking down into my hair as I lie there. He kisses me again quickly and then he's moving to the door. Ruby walks in, jumping out of the way for Asher.

"Hey. She's good?" I hear her whisper. Asher murmurs back but I can't make out the words.

"Are you sure you should be in there?" I hear Ruby ask.

Asher answers and then leaves. Ruby looks after him for several moments before turning to me with a huge smile. I love that I have two watchdogs. Asher and Ruby, both willing to ask the hard questions and put a wall between me and whatever might harm me. She's only asking because she loves us and wants the best for us.

"There's barely room for a girl to sit in here," she says dryly, coming into the room and spinning around. Already, there are several bouquets from various influential people at the hospital. My favorite is a huge vase of daisies from the surgical floor. Those nurses are still my friends, even though I've been on medical leave for awhile now.

"Just wait 'til I get to recovery," I drawl, appreciating the moment of humor to calm my nerves. "Flowers as far as the eye can see."

"Like a fucking Dutch flower field." Ruby grins at me, her eyes full of mischief. "Though I have a feeling Asher will make sure they're all your favorite. Red roses everywhere."

"Will you stay?" I ask, suddenly serious.

Ruby grabs my hand and squeezes tight. "I'll be here the whole time, down at the chapel. Asher will cover the surgery, I'll cover you in the spiritual realm."

"Thank you." My voice is barely a squeak, nerves and emotion closing off my throat. "I love you."

"And I love you, Nic. You're my girl, so don't go dying on

me. I'm an ugly crier. You can't do that to me. I'd never find a man."

And so I'm smiling as the team comes in to wheel me off to the operating room. The overhead lights whiz by and nurse friends line the hallway, all wishing me a successful operation and a speedy recovery. The sendoff is sweet with all the support they're giving me. I have to think most of it is genuine and not just because of my fiancé's last name. Just as the doors are swinging shut and the operating theater swallows me whole, it occurs to me that Asher's parents didn't come by to see me off.

With a giggle, I think I'll have to live just to piss them off.

"You sure look chipper," says Rosebud Memorial's best anesthesiologist. He's flanked by two assistants from the big city, here on Asher's dime to make sure I get the absolute best care. They make quick work of getting me strapped to the gurney and settled comfortably.

"Not every day you get a new lease on life," I quip back.

I'm ready.

I barely feel the IV prick my skin. Warmth flows through my veins quickly and Asher's face appears above me like an angel, backlit by the huge globe lights attached to the ceiling. He tells me he loves me.

And then...it's lights out.

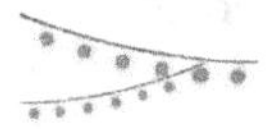

BLINDING LIGHT, floating.

I'm being sucked backward by a force I can't see. My long hair is obscuring my vision, a tangle of strands that threaten to choke me. I don't know where I am, but I know what's happening to me like I know my name is Nicole.

I'm dying.

I don't see my body lying there on the operating table. I don't see the loved ones who've died before me. I don't feel panic or fear or pain. I'm just...observing. Floating. Voices echoing off walls that don't exist. Shouts, then quiet, then more murmurs. All muffled and indistinguishable.

And then it all shifts. Light is sucked out and darkness sneaks in like a mist, swirling, thick, and sticky. It coats everything, turning the carefree floating into a heady thrill ride. My heart rate picks up, and though I can't see or hear or feel, I know I am stronger than before. This is not death. It's not life either. It's the something else. The thing we don't want to turn our eyes to. The thing we don't acknowledge because we can't explain it.

The in-between.

I suck in a breath, the mist stinging my lungs and surging blood through my veins and then...

It's all gone.

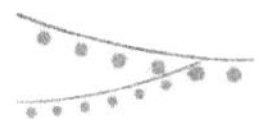

BEEP.

Beep.

Pain. Dear God, the pain.

My eyes shoot open and I attempt a gasp. Machines beep faster and a nurse with her back to me spins around and places a hand on my shoulder.

"Relax, Nicole. You're just waking up from surgery. Everything was a success. The tube is down your throat, so just relax for me."

Her words are efficient but not without feeling. I close my eyes again and do just what she said. Intense relief makes tears burn in my eyes. I made it. I lived. I have a new heart.

I drift back to sleep listening to the beeps of the machines tracking my new heart. It's the sweetest music I've ever heard.

WHEN I AWAKE the next time, the tube is gone from my throat and familiar faces line my room. Asher, Ruby, my surgeon, Dr. Harbell, and several of the surgical nurses. Asher, seeing my eyes now open, rushes to my side and carefully takes my hand in his. An IV is taped to the back of my hand, but he manages to sweep his thumb across my unmarred skin, warming me instantly.

Dr. Harbell walks over, smiling. "You're our model patient, Nicole."

I want to smile back but it's like I've forgotten how. I feel like part of a machine with lines running to various other parts, being kept alive by the mothership. Things are beeping steadily behind my head.

I'm drifting through time numb, in more ways than one, something I am very thankful for. I know the pain will come soon enough.

"We've taken out the breathing tube, so that's got to feel more comfortable. If you keep on this recovery pace, you'll be out of here before the normal two weeks. Any pain right now?"

My head feels as grounded as a helium balloon as I slowly say no. My voice is scratchy, barely recognizable.

Dr. Harbell pats my leg beneath the layers of blankets and the compression devices strapped to my calves. "You're in good hands, then. I'll be back tomorrow to check on you." His white coat sways with importance as he leaves the room.

Asher leans in and kisses my forehead. "Hi, darling. Welcome back."

My eyes trace his every movement but I feel like I'm held in a web of cotton balls, unable to speak or move or say much of anything. My brain is barely firing. God, he is handsome. Far too good looking to be stuck inside my hospital room all day long.

Ruby comes over to the other side of the bed and grins at me. "Thank you for saving me from the ugly cries. Now get to work healing so we can go back to pickleball, will you?"

I blink slowly, knowing she's being funny but unable to even think about laughing right now. My rib cage feels like a cement cast. I fear one wrong move or too deep of a breath will crack right through it, letting in a flood of pain.

"Sleep, darling. One of us will stay with you at all times," Asher whispers. It's all the permission I need to close my heavy eyelids and slip away.

*10 DAYS after surgery*

"ARE YOU EXCITED?" Ruby squeals, clapping her hands and bouncing on the tips of her tennis shoes.

I look up from the side of the hospital bed and force my face to mirror her expression. She's happier when I smile.

"So excited," I manage. The pain medicine makes my limbs feel like they're weighed down with lead. But without a steady stream of those meds, the pain and soreness make my breath hitch. Plus the nausea kicks in and then I'm throwing up the terrible hospital food, which also hurts my ribs. So I've chosen to stay numb.

"All right, let's get you standing and then into the wheelchair, hon," the older nurse declares as she bustles into the room. "I gave Asher a rundown of all the meds and when you need them. I also made him promise to call me on my personal cell phone if he runs into any trouble."

I nod gratefully. Not because she's kissing ass, but because being kind means I get out of this place. Ten whole days of being a patient and I'm ready to tear my hair out. Physical therapy got me up and walking one day out from surgery. My whole body was sore from that, which is weird because it was just my heart that got operated on. The immunosuppressants are playing nice with my body chemistry, which means I won't be rejecting my new heart anytime soon. If I could just get one goddamn night of uninterrupted sleep, I feel like I could wake up a whole new woman.

Ruby holds on to my arm as I stand from the bed. I give myself a moment to let the slight dizzy sensation recede before I attempt to walk to the wheelchair an orderly just brought in.

"Asher is just outside. Ol' Weathersfield got ahold of him," Ruby mutters. The nurse snorts softly.

Everyone knows what a pain in the ass Weathersfield is. He was chief of medicine here before Asher's father. He's been retired for over twenty years but he sometimes forgets that fact and thinks his opinion holds weight around here still.

I feel the seat of the wheelchair behind my knees and gratefully sink into it. "You'd think he could let go of my fiancé long enough so he can help me get home after open heart surgery," I grouse, feeling a little sorry for myself.

Ruby sweeps behind me to arrange my hair, which I'm

sure looks the worst it's ever looked. They didn't exactly use salon-grade products in the hospital. Plus all the crazy dreams I've been having on these pain meds has made my hair worse than a rat's nest.

"Let's go out there and give him the stink eye." Ruby elbows the orderly out of the way and pushes my wheelchair out the door. I suck in a deep breath, already feeling like I can breathe easier outside of that damn room.

Asher is down the long hallway at the bank of elevators, Weathersfield's weathered hand gripping his elbow. Asher looks our way, his gaze furious. He quickly smooths out his expression before turning back to Weathersfield. A moment later, he's headed our way, a big grin on his face.

"There's my girl. Ready to go home?"

He leans down to give me a hug. I can see Weathersfield over Asher's shoulder, still by the elevators. He's glaring at us. Before I can tell myself not to, I lift the hand that's wrapped around Asher's back and extend my middle finger.

Ruby gasps and jumps between us, like she suddenly needed to help me rearrange my feet on the pedals of the wheelchair. Asher releases me and I look toward the elevators. Weathersfield is nowhere to be seen.

Somewhere in my brain I know I should feel bad about my immature response, but I feel nothing inside. Thank you, pain meds.

"How does takeout from Cavender's sound? We can tuck you in on the couch and light a fire."

I reach up and take Asher's hand as Ruby pushes me down the hallway and out the door to Asher's waiting truck.

"Sounds like heaven."

The two fuss over me until I'm buckled and the passenger door is shut. I wave to Ruby as Asher puts the truck in drive. Thankfully, Asher doesn't see Weathersfield in his car as we exit through the hospital parking lot, but he certainly sees us.

His glare is just as angry as before, and a cell phone is now jammed to the side of his head.

I close my eyes and congratulate myself on being discharged. There really is no place better for recovery than home.

# CHAPTER THREE

It clings to me, cutting off my air and making the panic rise quickly in my chest. I look to the right and the whole world shifts in slow motion, solid tree trunks bending and morphing like flimsy Play-doh. Their canopies block the sun, leaving everything below in shadow.

It's happening again.

I know it, but I can't seem to stop it. I try to run—to where is a mystery because nothing in this dream world seems safe—but my legs don't work properly. The black fog on the ground seems to suck me in.

I feel hot breath against the back of my neck and I freeze.

"Quit fightin' it, darlin'," comes the southern drawl.

I swirl around. No one's there.

Goose bumps line every inch of my skin. I heard that. I heard a man's voice in my ear. It was low and gravelly, as dark as the mist around my ankles. I've heard it twice now, though the first time I couldn't make out the words. I've dreamed of this misted forest more times than I can count, and I'm sick of it.

"Who are you?" I yell, my voice coming out soft and pitiful.

I spin around again.

"Leave me alone!" I yell again, this time putting everything I have into it.

I'm jostled by invisible hands. Another scream curls in my throat but I'm suddenly blinking my eyes open to see Asher standing over me. Another blink and our bedroom materializes behind him. The vase of red roses always catches my attention. Asher has been replacing the blooms with fresh ones every week.

"Nicole," Asher says, concern etched across his face. He drops down and pulls me into a hug. "It's okay. I've got you. It's just a bad dream."

He rocks me while my breaths even out, my new heart slowly returning to a healthy rhythm. When I've composed myself, I pull back and Asher hauls me into his side to sit up in bed, my back to the solid wood headboard.

"Same one?"

I notice he's fully dressed and showered, the scent of soap and cologne clinging to him. One look at the bedside clock tells me I'm late to wake up this morning. Normally, it wouldn't matter. My days are filled with physical therapy torture and nurse visits. Or Jessica, the caretaker Asher hired, pushing me to eat more and get out in the sunshine to speed my recovery.

But today, Josephine is coming to visit.

I must look the part, no matter how tired I still am. No matter the ache in my ribs or the panic that sets in when I feel my heart race faster than it should. Ten weeks separate me from my day of surgery. Seventy days of focusing my efforts on recovering. My full-time job now is to regain the life I should have had, had it not been for being born with a faulty heart.

"Yeah, same thing as usual." I don't mention the man's voice or what he said. I don't need Asher any more concerned about me than he already is. The poor man has been doing double duty, running the hospital and playing nursemaid to me.

Asher opens his mouth to respond, but his phone vibrates in his pocket, pulling our attention. He releases me and slides the phone out. His face lights up.

"Mother's here early."

It takes every ounce of strength I have to school my face into a pleasant smile. Inside, I'm screaming, wishing I could send her to my misty forest and leave her there forever.

"I better get ready," I say demurely, hoping he can't feel the way my heart rate has climbed just knowing that woman is near.

Asher kisses my forehead and stands, hovering as I get out of bed and to my feet. "You look beautiful just the way you are, darling. Mother will be so happy to see your progress."

Like hell, she will. She was probably hoping I'd die right there on the operating table, which I almost did. It took weeks before Asher informed me that I coded in the middle of the surgery. He was probably correct to not tell me right away. Recovery was hard enough without knowing I nearly left this plane of existence.

"I can't wait to visit with her," I lie.

Asher leaves after he's assured I don't need his help to get dressed and do my hair. As I look at my sallow appearance in the mirror in the bathroom, I realize I need to be more posi-tive. I'm lucky to be alive. Lucky to have received a heart that assures me a chance at a long life. Lucky to have such a devoted fiancé.

I run a brush through my hair and make a mental note to ask Ruby if she has time to take me to the hairdresser soon. I could use a cut and color to get me looking like my old self. We've been careful to limit visitors during my recovery. Risk of infection is high after an invasive surgery. The immune suppressants I take to avoid rejection of the new heart mean that I will catch every cold and flu that someone brings into my environment. But I'm sick of staring at the four walls, even if this house is more beautiful than anything I lived in growing up.

Sadly, visiting with Josephine is not what I had in mind for expanding my horizons, but I'll have to put on a good front. Asher loves her and I love Asher.

"There you are. I was afraid you were going to sleep the day away," Josephine says as I enter the family room where she and Asher are chatting on the couches.

"As she should," Asher is quick to interject, standing up. "That surgery is one of the hardest to recover from. Nicole is one strong woman."

I come to his side and kiss his cheek, grateful for his support in the face of the dragon—I mean, his mother. Then I step over to Josephine, who does not stand up. We do the air-kiss thing that she prefers, even though I find the whole ritual pretentious. I move back to Asher's side as soon as possible and sink into the couch. He wraps his arm around my shoulders immediately.

Josephine launches into the next fundraiser she wants Asher's support on, ignoring him when he gently suggests that now is not the best time for him to be dividing his attention any further than it already is. Like the manipulator she'd deny with her dying breath, Josephine quickly diverts the conversation to a new topic, one that she can lavish praise on Asher, thus making him feel like he needs to do whatever his mother wishes because she's his biggest fan. It's classic manipulation by a narcissist, but Asher doesn't see it that way.

It's hard to see things for what they are when they've always been normal for us.

"Coffee, anyone?" The assistant Asher hired for me is standing in the room, looking highly uncomfortable with a heavy tray of coffee and cookies in her hands.

Asher bounds to his feet and takes the tray from her, placing it on the coffee table between our couches and thanking her for her kindness. Jessica blushes under his praise and backs out of the room. Knowing Josephine's hawk eyes are on me, I refrain from rolling mine. I understand why the young woman is blushing and stammering around my fiancé. I felt much the same way for the first year Asher and I dated.

"Let me just get the heavy whipping cream you like, Mother." Asher follows the same path as Jessica.

Josephine leans forward and takes a cookie from the pile, placing it on a small plate, which she holds in her lap. I brace for the first criticism, which I know will be coming shortly. It always does when Asher's head is turned away.

"My son is looking tired."

Ah. She thinks my recovery is too hard on Asher. No question as to how I've been. Just a concern that my near death might be stressing out her precious son.

"I'll see to it he goes to bed at a reasonable hour this week," I say meekly, leaning forward to select a cookie.

"You shouldn't be eating that, Nicole," Josephine snaps. "You wouldn't want to damage that brand-new heart."

I pull my arm back to see her smiling at me. Not warmly. Josephine doesn't know how to do that. Her long, thin face is twisted into what I imagine Disney modeled the wicked step-mothers in their stories after.

I smile, despite the vitriol that drips from this woman's mouth. *Hurry back, Asher.*

"You're right. What was I thinking? Must be the medications making my head fuzzy."

"Maybe you should lie down, dear." One thin eyebrow attempts to climb her forehead. It only serves to make her look more evil.

I surge to my feet, anger flooding through my veins like a tsunami. "Maybe I shall," I snap, unable to contain my irritation.

Asher chooses that moment to come back in the room with a small porcelain dish of cream. He takes in the scene, his pleasant expression turning to one of concern. "Are you feeling okay, Nicole?"

I nod, moving around the coffee table to ease up on my toes and kiss his cheek. "I'm fine. Just need a nap before the physical therapist comes by for my appointment. Plus I'm sure you'd like some time to visit with your mother."

Josephine's face is back to being one of serene peace, a look I know she's practiced all these years in various board-rooms and ballrooms. Perhaps I need to practice more.

Or invest in more Botox.

It takes me longer than it should to calm down and fall back asleep. Though my heart's doing well and the doctors are happy with my recovery, my stamina is still lagging. Naps are not an unusual thing for me, even ten weeks out from surgery.

When Asher wakes me some time later, he seems distracted. His hand rubs the back of his neck while he waits for me to sit up. I push my hair away from my face and stretch the kinks out.

"Is something wrong?"

Asher turns to me. "Did you tell Mother that you want me to not hover so much?"

My mouth gapes open. "No! No, I didn't say that at all."

Asher frowns, his dark eyebrows nearly pressed into a single line. "Are you sure? She said you went on and on about how tired I am lately and that my presence here at the house is hampering your recovery. She said you told her it's time for me to go back to work full-time."

I snap my mouth shut. Visions of my hands wrapped around Josephine's neck come unbidden. My fingers turn white while her neck takes on a red hue. She sputters and gasps, shock replacing that hideous frown. It's so real I have to squeeze my fists together to remind myself that I'm here in my bedroom with Asher.

What am I thinking? I don't have the strength to strangle a grown woman to death! I give my head a shake. Don't have the *strength*? I nearly laugh at the thought. Actually would have laughed out loud if it wasn't so ghastly. I would *never* strangle someone, whether I was at my full strength or not.

Standing, I slide my fingers into Asher's hair and then rest my hands on the back of his neck. I don't care about that woman. I care about my fiancé.

"Asher, honey," I whisper, standing on tiptoe to press my lips against his. With a groan, he slides his arms around my waist and holds me to his strong chest. I break away just long enough to assure him, "I want you with me all the time. You being here by my side is a gift."

He plucks another kiss from my lips. "Are you sure?"

I press myself even closer. "I'm very sure. In fact, I wanted to talk to you about getting an opinion from a new doctor."

At this, Asher pulls his head back, eyeing me cautiously. Nervously. "Why? Is something wrong?"

I gaze up at him with all the love and affection I feel shining through. I love this man with my whole, brand-new heart.

"I'd like to consult someone from obstetrics. A doctor used to high-risk pregnancies." I shoot my love a smile I feel all the way to my toes. "I'd like to find out how soon it's safe for me to get pregnant."

Asher swoops me back into his arms, his face buried in my hair. His voice is trembling when he answers. "I'd like that very much too."

# CHAPTER FOUR

It's been a hell of a long year.

All the excitement of having a new heart and a fresh outlook on life tends to fade in the face of constant physical therapy appointments, doctor visits, and the timing of handfuls of daily medications. It's been a marathon, not a sprint, and I am pleased to be back in the hospital to work, not as a patient.

I can't visit with patients one-on-one yet, or maybe ever, due to the immunosuppressants I'm on, but I'm back to having a purpose. I mostly chart for the surgical floor and oversee dosages and schedules on a part-time basis. It's a position made specifically for me, more than likely because my last name is about to be Kingsley. Part of me wants to fight back and not accept coddling, but I'm too happy to be out of the house to give this up.

"Yo, Nic," Ruby says as she sits on my desk. She's in scrubs, probably fresh from a surgery based on the way she still has mask marks on her cheeks and bridge of her nose. She's still stunning with her raven-black hair and green eyes.

"Just like old times. I'm working and you're just sitting

around," I quip. We both know that's not true. Ruby is the hardest worker I know.

She grins at me, too happy to see me back at work to dish out the teasing. I wish she would though. Everyone still walks on eggshells around me, worried that one joke or cross word will be too much stress for my new ticker.

She folds her hands around the knee that's crossed over her other leg. Her nails are painted bloodred. "I think your first day back calls for celebration. How about mocktails at Delario's after work?"

I lean in, dropping my voice. "Make it a real beer and you're on."

Ruby's eyes go wide. "Girl, you know I can't let you do that. No alcohol for you because of your meds. Ever."

I tilt my head, ready to beg. Nothing sounds better than a frosty cold beer right now. "Come on. Just a light one. Just a few sips."

Ruby sighs. "I don't know, Nic. Asher might kill me."

I waggle my eyebrows. "What Asher doesn't know won't kill him. Or you."

"Damn, girl. That year of rest and relaxation did you some good."

I roll my eyes. We both know it wasn't R & R. She was there with me every step of the way, making me do my exercises and getting me out of the house as much as possible with my limitations. She and Asher were my personal care team for three hundred and sixty-five days. I've put up with more pain and stress than any one person should have to deal with. I'm due a little bit of fun.

"Seriously. I'm a grown adult, I can drink if I want to," I snap, irritation at being watched over like a child.

Ruby draws her head back, holding her hands up. "Okay, okay. Sorry, babe. Just trying to watch out for you."

I instantly feel bad for snapping at her.

"I'm feeling good, Rub." I grab her hand and she squeezes it back.

"All right. Delario's today will be our little secret." And then she's gone, hips swaying as she waltzes down the hallway. More than one male's head swivels to watch her go.

I ONLY ENDED up drinking half of a light beer with Ruby and yet I feel the buzz in my head, reminding me of my college days when money was tight but everything was fun. I'm still well below the legal limit, but being without alcohol for so long before and after surgery has made me a lightweight.

The gorgeous house Asher and I bought together after our second year of dating is dark. The streetlights are on, but clearly Asher isn't home yet. This is not unusual as the man works incredibly hard. The garage opens when I press the button on the visor of my Mercedes-Benz.

This house has always made me giddy. It's over four thousand square feet with more bedrooms than I know what to do with. The green grass in the front is only topped by the sparkling pool in the backyard. I could never have afforded something so nice on my nurse's salary. Before my heart gave out for good and I had to go on medical leave, I insisted on paying the utilities. Even that took most of my paycheck.

I slam my door closed and round the hood. The neighbor's dog next door starts barking his head off at the noise. I shake my head. They've been leaving the dog out more and more recently. What's the point of having a dog if you're never home to play with it? I hit the button for the garage and the door slowly lowers, taking with it the sound of the barking dog.

I get started making dinner, assuming Asher will be home eventually. Something I refuse to do is constantly check on his whereabouts and demand when he'll be home. You either trust each other or you don't, is my motto in relationships. And I trust Asher. Full stop.

The barking continues when I take a plate of raw chicken out to the barbecue in our backyard. While the grill heats up, I do my best to look between the slats of the fence line that separate our yard from the neighbor's. Not one light is on in their house. The German shepherd paces along the fence, aggressively barking now that I'm closer. It suddenly jumps up and hits the fence with its front paws, startling me. I jump back and head for the grill, heart racing.

An hour later, I've eaten my grilled chicken and salad. And that infernal dog is still barking. I swear it's echoing in my skull, driving me crazy. I think about calling animal control, but I know they won't remove an animal from its home unless there's blatant abuse. The last thing I need is the neighbors knowing I called animal control on them.

I'm getting ready for bed and seriously wondering where Asher is when I can't take the barking anymore. I step outside and shout at the thing.

"Shut up!"

He pauses for a beat, and I have a sliver of hope that maybe he'll listen. Then he barks again with renewed vigor and all hope is dashed.

"Stop! Barking!" I yell, walking closer, emboldened by the fence between us. I can feel my heart pounding faster than it should, but it's like I can't do anything but feed the rage that's consuming me. How inconsiderate of my neighbors to just leave a loud animal out all day and night!

As if to show me just how little I matter, the dog jumps up on its hind legs and barks over and over again, it's nose just barely showing over the fence line.

If I had a shotgun, I just might shoot the damn thing for some peace and quiet. And then I get a better idea. An idea that won't land me in trouble, but will still solve the problem. Healthcare workers utilize this approach all the time. In fact, it's humane. I smile at the shadow leaping against the fence, my heart instantly calming at my idea.

I spin on my bare feet and march back inside, headed straight for my stack of medicine. I hate the feel of heavy-duty pain meds, so after I came home from surgery, I got off of them as soon as possible. Which means I have a half-full bottle of them at the back of the linen closet. Opening the bottle, I pour three capsules in my palm, then tilt out two more.

Back in the kitchen, I grab an organic, grass-fed sausage from the refrigerator and slice it down the middle. One by one, I empty the capsules' content into the sausage boat until it's full. Then I pick it up carefully, head back outside and face the nightmare of a dog.

"Time for bed, Cujo," I tell him softly. I can't remember his name, and honestly, it doesn't matter. Did the dog have any consideration for me? No. It was time to do what the owners should be doing.

I bend down and slide the loaded sausage between the slats, snatching my hand back when he instantly grabs it with his razor-sharp teeth. I look through the wood slats, just barely able to see him gobble it up in just a few bites. He's back to barking less than twenty seconds later, but I grin now as he barks away.

I probably should have looked up how much morphine a German shepherd can ingest without dying, but I honestly don't care the outcome as long as I get some peace and quiet. Before long, his barks get fewer and far between. He slumps down to the grass, his tongue lolling out the side of his mouth.

"Nighty night," I tell him. I thought I might feel some remorse, but all I feel is relief.

I head inside to enjoy my evening. I make sure to clean up the mess I made, flushing the empty capsules down the toilet and putting the pain meds in the back of the linen closet again.

Asher comes home thirty minutes later, looking tired but so handsome it takes my breath away. I reheat the chicken I grilled and plate it for him.

"You're an angel," he murmurs, kissing my cheek and taking a seat at the oversized kitchen island. "What have you been doing this evening?"

I skip over my time with Ruby at Delario's. I don't know his every move. He doesn't need to know mine. "Just doing a bit of research on the best florists in town."

Asher's face lights up. He dabs a napkin to his lips and swallows before commenting. Always the best manners. "Back to planning our wedding?"

I sit on his lap and play with his hair while he continues to eat. "I know the doctor said I need at least a year under my belt before we can try to have a baby. I figure if we do a small wedding in the spring, we can be pregnant by summer."

He puts down his fork and spins on the barstool, his arms around me. "I love that timeline. As long as it's not too much stress for you. I can hire a planner to take care of all the details. I notice you've been a little..."

I frown. "What?"

Asher smiles at me patiently. "Just a little snappier, moodier, than normal. Which is understandable with all you've gone through," he rushes to add. "I just don't want our wedding to be a source of stress."

He's not wrong. I have been a little moodier. Definitely displaying a shorter temper. But who wouldn't after the surgery and all I've done to recover?

I slide my fingers through his hair, determined to not let stress get the better of me going forward. With the buzz of alcohol still in my system, I press myself against him and whisper in my fiancé's ear.

"Take me to bed."

He does, showing me that even though he's tired, he always has time and energy for me.

I show him how not-stressed I am, keeping my words soft and my body even softer.

And not once during the night does a barking dog interrupt my sleep.

# CHAPTER FIVE

*B*right lights threaten to blind me. Asher's arm holds me even tighter against his side. I lift my nose in the air, giving everyone my good side, and smile for all I'm worth. The ballroom isn't as beautiful as last year, namely because of the cloying scent of lilies and chrysanthemums Josephine ordered from the florist. She found out red roses are my favorite and suddenly they no longer show up at any of the social events she organizes. I wonder if she knows she ordered a whole lot of funeral bouquets...

At least this year I'm not worried about the indents from the oxygen tubes being seen on my cheeks. The photographers at the hospital's annual fundraiser are aggressively trying to get a picture of Asher and me before he drops me off at his parents' table and gives his speech. My illness, our engagement, and his position at the hospital has become something of a viral story. One newspaper write-up in the *Grove Daily* and suddenly we were fielding requests for interviews at national news stations.

I'm proud of us for keeping our heads down and focusing on the life we want to build. Asher is doing a fantastic job as chief of medicine. I'm healing right on schedule. Our wedding in a couple months at the Kingsleys' summer cabin will be intimate and everything we want, despite Josephine making snarky comments about not inviting English royalty. I don't know who she thinks she is, but Rosebud Grove is a small town. She may think she's queen of Rosebud, but her kingdom is small in the grand scheme of things.

We make our way into the ballroom where Asher looks at me adoringly before kissing my cheek and depositing me into a chair at the head table. Then he quickly bounds up the stairs and walks across the stage. He belongs in the spotlight with his confident walk, the lopsided grin that makes everyone love him, and his American good looks. It's the one thing Josephine and I can agree on.

"Welcome, ladies and gentlemen!" Asher begins after the applause dies down enough to allow his voice to be heard over the sound system.

"Your scar is showing!" Josephine hisses in my ear, distracting me from the first part of Asher's speech.

She's not wrong. As I've healed, I've put on some of the weight I lost while sick. Asher doesn't have a single problem with the way the added pounds have mostly gone to my hips and breasts. When I picked out the gown for tonight's event, I ran it by Asher first. My healthy flesh is pushed up to create alluring cleavage, which also exposes the top two inches of the scar that runs down the middle of my chest. It's still pink though I know it'll eventually fade to silver. Asher agreed with me that the dress is perfection on me and that I shouldn't feel the need to hide my scar. It actually took a lot of courage for me to be seen in such a public arena with my imperfections on display, and before I sat down next to the devil, I was proud of myself.

Anger, hot and bright, takes over my good senses. Two can play this game, and I'm finally feeling well enough to play.

"Your rudeness is showing!" I snap back.

Josephine's head reels back so far I'm sure she's given herself whiplash. Her spine straightens and she looks away from me. We both listen to the rest of Asher's speech, fuming.

Maybe I should have waited until we were in a less public place to finally stand up for myself, but I've simply reached my limit with her catty comments. As Asher steps away from the podium to have a seat and eat our meal, I prepare myself for retaliation.

It doesn't take long to present itself. After the final dinner plate is cleared from our table, I excuse myself to go to the restroom. Josephine is waiting for me after I flush and exit the stall. I glance around quickly, seeing that the dimly lit bathroom is cleared out. Not one woman is touching up her makeup in the gilded mirrors or frantically texting on the velvet couch in the waiting area. I wash my hands, keeping an eye on the old bat.

"Can I help you?" I ask, my tone making it clear I don't intend to do anything to help her.

She storms over, the beaded gown she chose in a horrific burnt orange making her complexion seem like she's got one foot in the grave. If only I were that lucky.

She's so close to me I can smell the salmon she chose for dinner. "You better watch yourself, little girl. I can turn Asher against you in a heartbeat. One more snarky word out of you and I'll do it."

I don't back down easily. Not anymore. Life is too short to be under this woman's thumb. I finally feel well enough to turn over a new leaf. "I'd like to see you try, old lady."

Instead of ramping up her attack, she changes course. Now she's smiling, and honestly it's more terrifying than her frown. Except, I don't feel terrified. I feel incensed. Pissed off like I've never been before.

I was already dealt a shitty hand being born with a hole in my heart and a single parent who couldn't afford to do much about it. But I've overcome that now. In fact, my life has turned around completely. I'm about to marry the love of my life, who happens to have more money than he knows what to do with, and start a family with him. I have a new heart, a new lease on life.

And this woman wants to try to ruin all that.

I don't fucking think so.

"You have no idea who you're messing with," she snaps.

Unfortunately, I snap too.

Before I can think it through, my arm darts out and I've got her bony wrist in my hand, squeezing so tightly she squeaks out in pain. All that physical therapy from the last year comes in handy right now. I feel her rapid pulse below my fingers. A rush of adrenaline coursing through me has me feeling like I could do anything right now. I am omnipotent. All knowing. Ready to exact my vengeance finally. I swear I'm high off of it.

Nose to nose, I look her in those dead brown eyes and see fear. Good. It's about time.

"I don't think *you* know who you're messing with, Josephine," I drawl as if we're just having a normal conversation over coffee and cookies. I squeeze her wrist just a smidgeon harder, the urge to squeeze until I feel a crack almost making me heady. My voice is rough now, unrecognizable, even to my own ears.

"One word to Asher about anything negative and I'll ruin *you*. I will have his babies, take his last name, and become the head of this family. I'll snatch that title right out from under your old, weak, frail nose. You may want to reconsider how you treat me. I'd hate to see you end up in a retirement home before you're ready."

And with that threat, I let her go.

She instantly grabs her wrist and rubs the reddened skin. I shoot her a wink and exit the bathroom without another word.

The adrenaline leaves me quickly, of course. By the time Josephine comes back to the table, I'm trembling. I've overexerted myself. And I'm just a bit terrified, to be honest. I just threatened Asher's mother. Physically assaulted her, if we want to speak truthfully. She doesn't look at me, nor does she immediately say anything to her husband or Asher. After ten long minutes where I'm sure she's going to throw me under the bus at any minute, I decide I can't stay here any longer. I take out my phone and text Ruby underneath the table.

*Me: Wanna get out of here?*
*Ruby: Thought you'd never ask. Meet me outside in five.*
*Me: Delario stop, then home?*
*Ruby: Only if you're feeling okay.*
*Me: I feel amazing.*

And it's true. I've recovered from my surgery. Asher and I are on solid ground with our relationship and plans for the future. And now I've put dear old Josephine in her place. Asher pushes his chair back and stands, holding out his hand. He asks if I'd like to make the rounds with him and I decline, stating that I'm feeling tired. He's instantly concerned.

"Let her rest, Asher," Josephine says dully. "In fact, I'm heading home myself." She stands and hurries out of the room without even waiting for her husband.

Asher nods, but seems perplexed. "Okay. Text me when you're home so I know you're okay?"

I look up at him and know that everything is going to be perfect. "You know I will. I love you."

Asher leans down and places a slow kiss on my lips. "And I love you, darling."

I turn to leave but a waiter has just come behind me to

replenish the water glasses. We collide and water sloshes over the carafe on his tray and splashes on my dress, sliding down my cleavage. Asher jumps into action and grabs a napkin. I can feel heads turning to see what the commotion is about at the head table.

"Get the fuck out of my way," I hiss at the waiter. His startled expression turns to embarrassment.

"Yes, ma'am. I'm so sorry." He hustles out of the ballroom.

My head is buzzing, knowing I've made a scene. I grab the napkin from Asher and dab at my chest, careful around my scar. It takes a second for me to notice, but I feel Asher looking at me. His head is tilted to the side, like he's trying to solve a puzzle.

"Are you all right, darling?"

My cheeks flame with embarrassment. I probably overreacted there. Not probably. I know I did, which is so unlike me. Just a few years ago I was that waiter, pulling extra jobs to help pay for nursing school.

"Sorry. Just...stressed. I guess. I should go find him and apologize."

Asher runs his hands down my arms, staring down into my face. "I know you said the wedding planning wasn't stressing you out, but I think maybe you should take a vacation or something. You haven't gone anywhere in over a year. You're due some time off. How about I call the travel agent and have her book you a flight to go see your father? After all, you didn't get to see him at Christmas last year or your birthday. What do you say?"

I open my mouth to argue I don't want to go anywhere without him and that I'm not stressed. But how else can I explain that outburst? Well, *two* outbursts tonight, but he doesn't need to know about the first one.

"Okay, I'd like that," I hear myself saying.

And that's how I find myself slightly hungover and at the

airport the next day, carry-on bag in hand. I didn't have the heart to tell Asher that my dad's not like normal family, not that Asher's family is normal either. My dad's just never been super supportive, and he didn't even bother to come visit me after my surgery. Visiting with him now might cause me more stress.

But dear ol' Dad is waiting at the curb when I land in Nevada, the same ancient truck he's had for close to two decades. The gun rack attached to the back window is empty at least. He climbs out when he sees me, wearing worn jeans, a plaid shirt, and a jean jacket. His belly has gotten bigger since I saw him last. Probably due to the cheap scotch he loves to drink every night.

"Hey, Dad," I call, stopping at the back of the truck.

He steps up onto the sidewalk and throws his arms around me, startling me. "Hey, pumpkin."

My eyes close and I breathe him in. He smells the same as when I was a little girl. Hair gel, soap, and motor oil. He pats my back a few times and pulls back, clearing his throat and picking up my bag to put it in the bed of the truck. Silence descends and it's like neither one of us knows what to say to bridge the gap between us. I'm not sure how we got here either, but him not visiting when I was recovering hurt my feelings. We're ten minutes down the road when he finally speaks.

"I was surprised to get Asher's text this morning with your flight info." He's got one hand on the wheel, the other on the window casing.

"Yeah?"

He scrubs a hand down his face, looking older than the last time I saw him. There's a little more silver threaded through his dark brown hair. Despite the distance between us, it makes me sad to see him aging.

"Well, yeah. Considering you wanted me to stay away so

badly, I was surprised you wanted to even see me."

I turn away from the windshield where I've been cataloguing the changes in my hometown. I'm so confused. "Wanted you to stay away?"

Dad glances at me, then back at the road. "Josephine said you were so angry with me for not supporting you financially through nursing school that you couldn't even speak to me. She told me you'd heal better after the surgery if I didn't come visit. Keep your stress low and all that. So I stayed away." He swallows hard. "You gotta know it killed me to stay away when I knew you were hurting like that."

My jaw feels like it's on the floorboards. "Josephine said that?"

He frowns, glancing at me repeatedly before pulling the truck over to the side of the road and turning to give me his full attention. "Yeah, Josephine. She said you didn't want my presence to ruin your reputation there in Rosebud."

My shock is quickly turning to rage. That woman is at the top of my shit list. Hell, she's the only one on my shit list.

I reach across the old bench seat and take my father's hand. His skin is weathered and littered with age spots.

"Dad. I never said any of that. I promise you. That old bat is making up stories to make my life hell."

Dad's eyes fill with tears. He lurches forward and pulls me into another rough hug that takes me back in time. "I love you, pumpkin. And I'm so proud of you."

I squeeze him back hard, brain spinning. "I love you too, Dad."

If I don't stop this woman now, she'll ruin my life. I know that for a fact like I know Asher is the man for me. I thought maybe I'd overreacted by grabbing her wrist and threatening her, but now I'm thinking I haven't taken it far enough.

When I get back, I'm going to put a stop to her once and for all.

# CHAPTER SIX

My visit with Dad was everything Asher was hoping it would be. We drank way more coffee than my new heart appreciated. We sat on his over-sized couch and reminisced for hours. Talked about my wedding and the future I had planned. I even got him to agree to come to the wedding and walk me down the aisle. It broke my heart a little to see him tear up when I asked him. To think that Josephine almost ruined my relationship with the only parent I had left. When he dropped me off at the airport, I knew I had him in my corner once again. I hadn't even realized how much I missed him until he wrapped me in his classic bear hug.

Back in Rosebud Grove, I haven't come up with a plan yet for how to deal with Josephine, but I decide I need Asher on my side. He can no longer be left in the dark about his mother's behavior. They say the best way to a man's heart is through his stomach. As a nurse, I don't give much credence to old wives' tales, but even so, I'm preparing his favorite meal of lasagna and garlic bread, planning to sit him down with a full belly and explain what's been going on.

The doorbell rings, startling me. I glance at the lasagna in the oven and decide it won't burn if I run off to get the door. I throw down the oven mitts and head for the front of the house. There's a dark shadow standing outside my door, shifting side to side. The hair on the back of my neck stands up, which has my stomach churning.

"Who is it?" I ask loudly, hand on the deadbolt, cursing the fact we don't have a doorbell camera I could check before opening the door. The frosted glass on either side of the door protects our privacy, but also doesn't allow me to see out. Rosebud Grove is so safe, it just didn't seem like a priority.

"Um, I'm Emily? Emily MacDonald?" The voice that answers back is young. A slight feminine twang.

I huff out a sigh of relief and unlock the door. I'm being ridiculous. It's probably some high schooler looking for donations. I swing the door open and blink in surprise. It is a woman on my doorstep, and while she's young, she doesn't look at all like she's southern because of what she's wearing. Baggy black cargo pants with a tight black long-sleeved shirt, black-and-silver spiked dog collar, jet-black hair I'm assuming is dyed based on the blond roots, and terrifying makeup.

"Hey," she says awkwardly, shifting in her thick black boots.

"Hello," I manage, stepping so my body is blocking the view into my house. That feeling of danger is back. I wish I thought to bring my cell phone with me. "Can I help you?"

The girl's fingers are twisting, her thumb nail chipping off the dark purple polish on her other fingers. Her breath is raspy, like she's smoked way too many cigarettes in her young life. "I, uh, read your story about your heart transplant."

"Oh, well, if you're with a media outlet," I begin, the idea of this girl being with a newspaper or news station feeling a bit ridiculous.

She holds up a hand, and I notice it's shaking. "No, I ain't.

I, um, I'm Emily. Emily MacDonald. I jus' had a transplant too. Lungs."

I lean into the door, now worried for her. Her lungs don't sound good. I don't need a nursing degree to know that. "Well, I'm glad to hear that. How are you feeling?"

She nods, acknowledging my question, but doesn't answer. "I had to come warn you. I think...well...I think someone is comin' for us."

My vision blurs around the edges, a shot of adrenaline making my fingers tingle. "I'm sorry, what?"

She darts a look over her shoulder before focusing those startling blue eyes back on me. I look over her shoulder too but don't see anything suspicious.

"Don' you feel it?" She leans in, and I try to put space between us. "That pull? That feelin' that takes over and the voice in your head ain't yours anymore?"

I'm officially freaking the fuck out. This girl is insane. My brain spins, wondering if I can slam the door fast enough and lock it before she can make her way inside. I remember that one training I took my first year on the surgical floor. We had to learn how to deal with irate patients, people out of their minds with pain and medication. Always talk them down, remove yourself physically, then call for the authorities.

"I'm sorry. I don't know what you're talking about, but I'm sure the police would help you if you feel unsafe," I say far more calmly than I feel. I shift my weight, readying myself to scoot back and slam the door shut.

Emily's eyes are haunting. Her pupils are dilated and I'm wondering what drugs she's on. Was her whole lung transplant story fake? She starts shaking her head, short hair flying around her face.

"No. You don't understand. I'm a professional hacker. I looked into the hospital and I know. I know what he did. And *you* did. You need to know what's goin' on!" Her voice is rising with each word, then she coughs violently, not bothering to cover her mouth.

Truly, she sounds insane. And the nurse inside me is worried about her breathing.

"He's..." she now whispers, moisture flooding her eyes.

I frown, afraid to look away but wishing her piercing blue eyes would look elsewhere. What does she know? What does she mean, what I did? Or what *he* did? Who's he?

"I think you need to go see your doctor, Emily," I say firmly, then use her distraction over the coughing fit to step back and slam the door. I flick the lock lightning fast, then lean against the door, listening for her. My heart is thundering in my chest. I force myself to take deep breaths to slow it down.

Emily's coughs subside and there's blessed silence. I listen for footsteps, now pressing my ear to the door. When I don't hear them, I pull my head away and realize I should have immediately gone for my phone to call 911. What if she goes around to the back of the house? Did I lock the back door?

I take one step in that direction and then freeze. I don't hear footsteps.

I hear a heavy thump.

Spinning back around, I see a dark shadow in the form of a body, slumped on my doorstep. She's not moving. I can't tell through the frosted glass if she's breathing. The nurse in me is screaming at me to go check on her.

"Shit, shit, shit," I chant, spinning in a circle.

This isn't my problem. Emily and whatever psychosis she has isn't my issue. But I can't just leave a girl passed out or potentially dying on my doorstep. I make my decision, running for the kitchen to grab my cell phone, then running back to the front door. I swing it open, braced for Emily to pop back up and force her way into the house, having tricked me.

She does none of those things.

She just lies there on her side, ragged breath piercing the quiet peace of our street. I drop into a crouch and roll her onto her back. Her forehead's bleeding, probably from not catching her fall.

"Emily?" I ask, shifting into nurse mode. I feel for a heart rate in her neck and find it. It's thready and fast. Her breathing now sounds like she's breathing through a straw. She needs oxygen right away.

I pull out my phone to call for an ambulance, but her hand grabs my wrist, her grip surprisingly strong.

"Shit!" I squeal. I didn't realize she had one eye slightly open, watching me. I push down the fear. "I need to get you to the hospital, Emily."

She shakes her head slowly. "You...don't...get it." Her breathing is so labored I'm scared she'll pass out again if she keeps trying to talk.

"Shh. Save your oxygen. I'll get the paramedics here in just a few minutes, okay?"

Her face has gone white as a sheet. It makes the heavy black eye makeup stand out even more. Her purple-painted lips tilt into a creepy smile.

"Comin'," she wheezes. I lean in, despite my fear, trying to understand her. She drops my wrist and I punch in the three numbers, calling for help. "For...all..."

"911, what's your emergency?" I hear a pleasant voice in my ear, but all my attention is on Emily.

"Of us...Nicole...Renee...Kelly."

Emily's head slumps to the side, the blood from her eyebrow dripping onto the fall welcome mat I put out just last week. Every ounce of panic freezes into a cold sheet of ice. She used my middle name. The one not even Asher knows about. I had it removed legally the day I turned eighteen, not needing the reminder of the mother who left me the day I was born. How would this mentally disturbed young woman know my full name?

"Well, shit," I mutter, putting the phone on speaker and setting it down on the brick floor my Emily's knees.

"Ma'am? What's the emergency?"

I feel her neck again and can't seem to find a pulse. My hands go into position over her chest to begin compressions.

"Early twenties female. Collapsed. No heart rate detected. Starting chest compressions. Need oxygen and defibrillator as soon as possible," I shout, hoping the operator can hear me. I give her my address next and she promises to send an ambulance.

I take a break from compressions to hang up the phone. I'm in position again, my hands directly over her rib cage when my brain clicks into gear. She said she's a hacker. She knew my old middle name. Could any of the other crazy things she said be true? Was someone actually after her? Who did she mean by all of us?

What the hell is going on here?

The sound of distant sirens breaks into my racing thoughts. I restart chest compressions, out of breath quickly and no closer to answers when the paramedics run up our walkway and take over. I give them all the details I know. It doesn't look good for Emily MacDonald. I somehow feel guilty when thirty minutes ago, I didn't know this girl existed.

By the time they whisk her away in the ambulance, sirens wailing and lights flashing in the night sky, Asher pulls into the driveway and my lasagna is burned. I'm shaking so badly not even his hugs and reassurance that I did the right thing can settle me down.

Before bed, Asher gets a call from the hospital that Emily didn't make it. For reasons beyond me, I'm...feeling a certain way about that news. Part of me is crushed at the loss of a human I interacted with during their last moments. Part of me is relieved that she and her crazy warnings are gone for good.

The confrontation about his mother is the last thing on my mind when I finally drift into sleep riddled with nightmares. Mostly, I relive Emily's final warning over and over again, not knowing what it means, but determined to do some digging so I can move on.

If someone was coming after her, what would make her come to me for help? What connects Emily MacDonald to me? Other than being two transplant survivors. There're thousands of us across the country, with more added to the list every day. Why me?

There's got to be more to this story.

# CHAPTER SEVEN

"Hey, Nicole." Barbara, the charge nurse on the surgical floor today, places a sheet of paper on my desk. She taps it with a sturdy no-nonsense finger. "I think you swapped patients on that cardiac inversion."

I lift my head from the computer where I've been zoning out for at least ten minutes when I should have been inputting patient records. She doesn't look mad about it, but a mistake like that shouldn't have been made. I minimize the screen and look at the paper, taking in the patient name that shouldn't be there. Shit. I did mess up.

"I'm so sorry, Barbara. Thank you for catching that. Let me fix it right away." I snatch the paper and crumple it, tossing it into the trash bin next to my desk.

I look up again when she doesn't leave right away. The sheepish part of me that knows I messed up remains silent. In its place is a part of me that wonders if she's going to make a big deal of it. Kingsley isn't my last name yet, but it will be in a few short weeks. She better watch her tone.

"Is everything okay, Nicole? You've seemed a little...off... today," she says kindly.

I dip my head, embarrassed anyone noticed my lack of focus. "I'm okay. Just a bit more tired than usual."

That's a lie. Absolutely nothing has been going on inside my head except wondering about the goth girl who died on my doorstep last night. I'm surprised I haven't messed up more patient records.

Barbara puts her hand on my shoulder. "Why don't you get something to drink from the cafeteria and get some fresh air while you're at it too?"

I accept her kind offer, though I'm not typically one to take the state-mandated fifteen-minute breaks. "You know what? I think that's a great idea. Thank you."

I stand, collect my wallet and phone and step around her. She doesn't say anything else and I know I have Asher's status to thank for it. Normally, an error that egregious would at least come with a stern verbal warning. Mistakes in the hospital setting can lead to death, so errors are taken seriously.

When I get to the end of the hallway and make a left, on my way to the emergency room instead of the cafeteria, a voice in my head reminds me that errors happen all the time. As the chief's future wife, they can simply look the other way. I roll my eyes. Like Barbara's never made a mistake before. Please. Now that I think about it, I don't feel so bad anymore. They're lucky I'm still here working at all when I could be home, living the housewife life.

The atmosphere in the ER is drastically more hectic than anywhere else in the hospital. My gaze darts around the chaos, looking for Dr. Shapiro, the ER doc on call who treated Emily. He should be just about done with his twenty-four-hour shift. I spot him a moment later coming out of a curtained-off patient area and head in his direction, darting around gurneys and nurses.

"Dr. Shapiro?" I call out, seeing him turn to walk in the

opposite direction. He stops and looks over his shoulder. When he sees me, he smiles and closes the cover on his iPad.

"Nicole. Nice to see you up and about. Everything okay?"

I nod, a little out of breath. All this stress is probably taking a toll on my new heart. "Yes, I'm good. I was actually wondering if you could tell me more about Emily MacDonald, the young girl who was transported here last night around nine?"

His expression turns serious. "I heard she collapsed at your house?"

I nod again. "I did CPR until the paramedics arrived."

He shifts us closer to the wall and out of the way of a transporter moving a patient in a wheelchair. "I'm sorry to tell you she didn't make it. Her body was already rejecting the new lungs. There was nothing you could have done. She should have been home in Los Angeles with her transplant team getting emergency care."

So she wasn't lying about the transplant. And she's from LA. I gather these tidbits like precious pearls. I look dutifully upset, pausing like most people would to absorb the news.

"I'd like to send her family some flowers. Do you happen to have her address? Or a middle name?"

Dr. Shapiro winces. "I can't give out that information." He glances behind me and then leans in closer. "But a Google search might tell you her middle name anyway. It's Quinn."

"Thank you," I murmur, placing my hand on his arm. "I won't forget your kindness."

I walk away, already feeling reenergized. I've never been happier to have the Kingsleys' good name to open doors and loosen lips. I head for the outdoor Zen garden Josephine fundraised for several years ago and have a seat on a wooden bench in the shade. I pull out my phone and search for Emily using her full name and Los Angeles as search terms. A whole list of websites pop up, that for a small fee, will tell me all about her basic information. I skip those and hit pay dirt on the second page of results.

Her Instagram profile.

It's a public profile which seems incongruent with being a computer hacker. Seems like she'd want to keep her life more private. Then again, maybe she knew any hacker worth their salt could get her private information whether she set her socials to private or not. I scan down the profile, seeing an insane amount of boba tea pictures. I can't understand some people's fascination with posting every meal they've ever eaten. I halt the scroll when I get to a picture of legs in compression socks in what looks like a hospital bed. The caption?

*Strange that someone's death will give me life. Thank you, science!*

I'm about to keep scrolling, hoping to find something that might explain her delusional warning, but freeze instead. I blink rapidly, heart beginning to hammer in my chest. There, below the picture, is the date it was posted.

Her lung transplant happened the same day I received my heart.

I glance up at the beautiful trees ringing this shady area, seeing absolutely none of it. What are the odds we had our transplants on the same day? Hers in Los Angeles, mine in Rosebud Grove.

That information spins around and around in my head, but no matter which way I position all the pieces of Emily MacDonald that I know about, nothing adds up to a complete picture. I'm just as lost as I was last night as she lay dying on my doorstep.

My phone pings, and I nearly drop it on the pavers at my feet.

*Ruby: Hey, where'd you go?*

She must have come by my desk and found me gone. I switch over to the texting app and tell her I'm on my way back to my desk. Before I stand, I go back to Instagram and screenshot what I've found. I'll study it later and see if I can find any other clues.

I brush myself off, dry swallow the heart pill I forgot to take this morning, and head back inside. I don't know why I'm so obsessed with this girl. She was probably high on drugs or mentally unstable. Her warnings were just the sad blathering of a confused girl. Maybe she saw my transplant story in the newspaper and felt a connection. Surgical procedures like the ones we'd both had were life changing and also isolating. Not many people her age would be able to relate to what she was going through. All of that could have caused her to want to reach out, to bond with me.

When I reach my desk, Ruby is still there, twirling around in my ergonomic chair just to piss me off. "Well, well, well. What do we have here? You cutting out on work already, Mrs. Kingsley?"

I roll my eyes and gesture for her to move. She hops to her feet, still smirking.

"I stepped outside to get some fresh air."

Her expression morphs to one of concern. I hate the way both her and Asher instantly become concerned whenever I'm anything but bursting with energy. I hate that I've given them reason to hover over me like mother hens. I desperately want to quit being the sick girl.

I hold up my hand to stop the barrage of questions. "I'm fine. Just a bit tired from last night's events."

Ruby nods, leaning against my desk. "I heard some rumors. Crazy girl collapsed and died on your doorstep? That would make anyone a bit stressed. Why don't you go home?"

I shake my mouse to wake up my computer. "I only work one day a week. And I took that day off last week to go see my dad. Pretty sure asking for more time off would be frowned upon."

Ruby scoffs. "You're Nicole fucking Kingsley. You do what you want, babe."

I shake my head and pull up the patient's record that I botched earlier this morning. "Not for a few more weeks."

"Oof. Speaking of Mrs. Kingsley. There's the old bat coming now." Ruby's looking over the partition of my cubicle.

I lift up out of my seat and spy Josephine at the other end of the surgical floor hallway, her hand in Mr. Weathersfield's elbow. They're pointing at things, probably finding fault everywhere and threatening nurses with being fired. God, they're annoying. We both duck down, now hiding in my cubicle.

"Think I could make a run for it and get out of here without them seeing me?" I hiss.

Ruby's nearly shaking with the effort to hold back laughter. "Not now. You're stuck kissing that old lady's ass."

I narrow my eyes, already pissed. I'm done kissing her ass. Actually, I haven't told Ruby about what happened at the fundraiser. I haven't seen her since I immediately went out to New Mexico to see my dad. Emily happened, and I kind of forgot I threatened my future mother-in-law.

"Mother! There you are."

Our heads whip back to each other, eyes wide. Sounds like Asher is on the surgical floor this morning too. I can't hear what they're saying, but their voices get fainter. Ruby finally lifts her head up and checks out the scene.

"They're gone," she says with as much relief as I feel. She stands back up and I check out the hallway just to be sure. "Did your man just save you again?"

I smile, thinking of how often Asher runs interference for me without even consciously doing it. He doesn't know the half of what that old bat has said to me. Maybe tonight I can tell him everything and get him to separate us even further from his mother. Well, I won't tell him *everything*. I'll conveniently leave out the part where I grabbed her wrist and threatened her. He doesn't need to know that part.

Ruby's phone buzzes and she reads the text message on the screen. "Shit, I have to go. Some of us have to stick to our fifteen-minute breaks."

I shove her as she turns to leave. She laughs, walking away and taking all her positivity with her. I turn back to my computer, willing my brain to focus on what I'm doing.

I end up having to stay late, thanks to my scatterbrain. The sun is already setting as I walk to my car in the parking garage. I hear a car alarm beep and look around. That's when I see her.

Josephine.

Alone, walking to her Mercedes, heels clicking on the concrete. I look around again, not seeing anyone else on this level of the garage. I dart behind a car and watch her. She's distracted, reading something on her phone. I dart around another car, keeping pace with her. I'm quiet, thanks to the tennis shoes I always wear to the hospital to work. I'm not pretentious like Josephine. Aren't her feet killing her in those heels?

The overhead light by her vehicle is out, allowing me to lurk in the shadows as she fumbles around in her large handbag, looking for her keys. I could so easily dash around this car, push her from behind and run away. She wouldn't see me coming or going. And in those heels at her age, unprepared for an attack, she'd probably go down hard. Might even hit her head on the concrete.

The smile on my face startles me. So does the pressing urge to do just that. Then I think of Asher and relax my muscles. I couldn't live with the guilt of killing his mother. Could I? Eliminating her would certainly take care of a lot of my problems though.

The engine of her car cranks over and she zooms out of

the garage, unaware of my presence or the fact that I just let her live. There must be cameras all over this place, a fact I didn't think of until just now.

But maybe, just maybe, if I caught her unaware in a much more private place...

Could I do it?

# CHAPTER EIGHT

I turn off my location on my cell phone, then set it down on the sticky tabletop. Delario's isn't a place Josephine would be caught dead in, which is one reason I love it. Their beer is always ice cold and no one from my new social circle would ever be here to spy on me and report back to Asher. Technically, I shouldn't be drinking alcohol, but one beer isn't going to ruin any of my progress. And it's the one last part of my prior life that I've kept. A girl can't live off fundraisers and tea and executive boards alone. She needs a place to blow off steam.

The server drops off two overflowing mugs of beer and leaves, off to take the order from the table in the back with a slew of rowdy linemen. The flicker of the neon sign hanging in the window by our table is giving the strobe-like effect of a nightclub.

Ruby takes a dainty sip. "Okay, spill it."

I hold up a finger and take my own swig, swallowing a quarter of the liquid before I set it back down with a smack. "God, I needed that!" Ruby smiles, but her head is cocked to the side. "What?"

"I don't know. You just seem...different."

"Different how?"

She shrugs. "I'm not sure. Just different. Anyway, tell me everything about this girl on your doorstep."

So I do. I tell her everything, even the parts I left out when I told the police and Asher what had happened. Ruby is just as stumped as I am. She's also concerned about Emily's vague threats, which validates how I've been feeling.

"What could that possibly mean? And what does it have to do with you?"

I shake my head and take the last sip of my beer. Damn. They always go down way too easy, but I should limit myself to one beer or it might interact with all the medicine I still have to take.

"I have no idea, Ruby. That's what I'm trying to figure out. That's where my brain's been the last few days. I can't seem to find much about her, but I also can't let it go." I lean in, dropping my voice though no one is listening to us. "She really freaked me out. She found my unlisted address and shows up on my doorstep unannounced with crazy warnings and then dies? It's creepy as hell! Does that make me a bad person? Being relieved she's dead?"

Ruby grabs my hand and squeezes tightly. "No, not at all. You know I'm a big believer in listening to your intuition. I wouldn't be alive if I hadn't listened to my own. If that girl creeped you out, you should probably stay far, far away. Drop whatever research you're doing on her. Like you said, she's dead. Let it go and move on with your life. For heaven's sake, your wedding is in three weeks!"

I nod, but I can't get myself to agree to let it all drop. I feel compelled to find out what she was rambling on about. Or at the very least, find out if she was mentally fit or not.

Ruby must see the conflict on my face. "Every time the courts contact me to get a statement on whether that son of a bitch deserves parole, I don't answer. Don't even open the envelope. You know why? Because all that shit's behind me, where it should stay. I only look to the future. I think you should too."

It's my turn to comfort Ruby. It took a whole year of friendship before she felt comfortable enough to tell me about the worst day of her life. When she was in nursing school, a man snatched her on her morning run, dragged her into the woods, and sexually assaulted her. She put up a fight and made a ton of noise. She fully believed the man intended to kill her afterward but got distracted when a truck drove near where he'd stashed her, perhaps responding to all the noise she made. She was able to get the duct tape off her ankles and made a run for it, trusting her instincts on which way to run. They didn't find the man who did this to her until he was arrested many years later for murder. The DNA samples matched up and she found her rapist.

"I think that's part of my problem," I say after she releases my hand and takes another swig of beer. "My intuition is swinging back and forth, one minute telling me to drop it and the next telling me to dig in. I'm not sure which to believe."

Ruby studies me for awhile. "As your friend, I don't want to see you stressed. After all you've been through, you deserve to ride off into the sunset with Asher and live a life of ease. But as a woman who trusts her intuition more than what's right in front of me, if there's a part of you that thinks you should investigate...I say do it. When you find out she was just a mentally disturbed individual, you can set your mind at ease, right?"

I nod, mind made up. "Okay."

Ruby grabs my hand again. "But if it gets to be too much, you come to me, okay? I'll help you put it aside or backtrack away from whatever you find. I'm your ride or die, babe."

I shove my chair back and reach over the table to pull Ruby into a neck-choking hug. "I love you," I whisper in her ear.

She hugs me back just as fiercely. "I love you too."

ASHER GETS HOME LATE that night like he always does. I sit next to him at the kitchen island while he eats the dinner I made earlier and set aside for him. This might be my favorite time of day, when we can sit in the dark and catch up. Just the two of us.

When he's done eating, I broach the subject I've been thinking long and hard about. I would never agree with Josephine, just on principle, but she may have a small point on this one topic.

"I was thinking about extending my medical leave again," I say quietly. She's been hounding me to quit, simply because of the terrible image of a Kingsley working a low-wage job.

Asher frowns, and I know right where his brain went. I hold up my hand.

"I feel fine, I promise. I just want to focus on the wedding full-time and not stress about a work shift." I lean in and kiss him, loving the way his scent wraps around me when I'm this close. Makes me want to snuggle into his chest and never leave. "Plus, as the chief's wife, I'm not sure I should be sitting in a cubicle doing data entry."

Asher smiles, one side higher than the other. "I like the way that sounds. I can't wait to call you my wife." He closes the gap and kisses me again, this time taking the kiss deeper. When he pulls back, we're both breathless. "I think you should just quit altogether, darling."

I slide off my barstool and sit on his lap. His arms come around me, holding me tight. "I don't want to give up my job entirely just yet."

Asher nuzzles my neck, his gaze dipping down to take in the silky nightgown I've taken to wearing now that I'm feeling so much better. "I'll support you in whatever you want. I just want you happy and healthy."

I run my fingers through the back of his hair and his hand slides under the hem of my nightie and up my thigh. "And I just want *you*. You and me. We can take on anything together."

Asher stands from the barstool, wrapping my legs around his waist before he carries us to the bedroom where it's just him and me and the love we have for each other. I quit taking birth control last month in hopes we'd get pregnant right away. Asher thinks we're waiting for after the wedding, but that can't come soon enough for me. He's my forever, and it's time we start working on that future.

When he's fast asleep awhile later, I lie there in the dark, staring up at the vaulted ceiling and listening to him breathe. I envision the life we'll have. The babies. The career. The local fame. We're already the golden couple, the term the newspaper gave us when they ran the article about my transplant. Imagine how much more we'll be revered when I get Josephine out of my way and give Asher a house full of children.

I've decided two things after talking with Ruby. I will investigate Emily MacDonald and find out if there's any validity to her strange warning about someone coming for us, whoever the *us* may be. And I'll investigate Josephine while I'm at it. Surely there's a skeleton or two in her closet that I can use to blackmail her into silence.

I refuse to let anything overshadow my marriage to Asher. I'm about to have everything I've ever wanted in this world, and I won't let either woman take that away from me.

Rolling to my side, I grab my cell phone off the bedside table and begin to search. If I need to, I'll hire a private investigator, but for now, I'll do it myself. I've got three weeks before the wedding and nothing but time on my hands.

# CHAPTER NINE

*I* head into the hospital the next morning after the nursing shift change, using my name badge to enter the building through the side entrance like I normally do. The whites of my eyes are a bit on the red side, and if one looks closely enough, they'll see the puffiness under them too. I stayed up way too late last night. When I finally went to sleep with almost nothing more than I already knew about Emily and Josephine, I decided I needed to be craftier. Good girls always finish last, isn't that right?

I nod and smile at a woman walking by who works in the transcription office. The astringent scent of the hospital is repulsive to some but only makes me feel at home. Between my medical condition and my job, I've spent more time in hospitals than I have in a house. Which is why I know medical records sometimes hold secrets that otherwise would never be found. Patient-doctor confidentiality hides a lot of sins.

Asher is at a conference in the city today, so I bypass the surgical wing where my coworkers might have a bazillion questions and head straight for his office. Helen, his administrative assistant, smiles warmly when she sees me approach. She's almost retirement age, having worked for Asher's father also.

"Well, good morning, Nicole. You're looking fantastic." She rounds her desk and gives me a hug.

She's a good liar.

I hug her back and plaster on the sweet smile she wants to see. "I wanted to surprise Asher."

Her smile dims. "Oh, I'm sorry. He's at a conference today."

I'm irritated that she thinks I don't know my own fiancé's schedule. I maintain my smile however. "Yes, he is. Which is why it's the perfect time to decorate his office." I shimmy the oversized bag I have slung over my shoulder.

Her grin is back and she even punctuates it with a wink. "That's so sweet! Head on in, but holler if you need any help."

"Thank you, Helen, but I know you're super busy. It's just some plants and pictures to warm the space up. You know Asher. Too busy to think of things like decoration."

We both laugh like old friends, and Helen heads back behind her desk, the phone already ringing. I swoop inside Asher's office, quietly closing the door behind me. I turn in a circle, taking stock of his office and putting my plan into action. I did, in fact, bring plants and pictures to put up in his office. I take a few out and place them around the room. I also move some furniture, purposely being loud so Helen knows I'm rearranging things. It's a bit chaotic, and somehow, the love seat in his office ends up in front of the door.

Once that obstacle is in place, I head for his desk where I sit quietly, firing up his computer. Not only do I know Asher's schedule, I know his login and passwords. There have been several times he's needed me to log in and look up a few things while he's been traveling. Unless he's changed his passwords, I should be able to get right in.

I carefully punch in his username and password, pausing only a second before hitting submit. In the second it takes to log him in, I hold my breath, worried alarms will start ringing like a winning slot machine in Vegas if I got it wrong. Thankfully, alarms don't ring and the computer opens to two screens: the hospital's database and Asher's work email. My relief is audible, but I quickly clamp my lips closed. I don't want Helen to hear anything through these thin walls.

Clicking quickly, I ignore his email and type in Emily's full name into the hospital database. There's nothing in our local hospital records apart from the ER visit to confirm her death, which makes sense. She lived four hundred miles away. It takes a few more clicks and a few more logins where I hold my breath, but I get into the national database for our hospital system. It's a long shot. There are quite a few hospitals in California where she could have been a patient, but Rosebud's parent company is known for transplants.

There it is.

Emily Q. MacDonald.

My fingers are trembling as I begin to frantically click open all the records. My eyes scan right and left, reading as much as I can as quickly as I can. This confirms she got her lungs the same day I got my heart. I have her surgeon's name, the notes from the surgery, and all her follow-ups. She was indeed having issues with rejection, which explains the list of her medications getting longer and longer. Could all of those medications have led to the delusion she displayed on my doorstep?

There's no mention of mental illness in her patient records, but that's not surprising. Patients with actual mental illness can be very good at hiding it. The last thing a young woman after transplant would want is more doctor appoint-ments added to her schedule, this time for psychiatric care.

There's nothing further in her medical records to explain her panic, so I close out of those. I re-read her operating room report and freeze on one mention. It's just a quick sentence. Probably had no meaning for the doctor when he recorded it.

*Lungs delivered still viable, even after a slight flight delay out of Live Oak County, Texas.*

My breath hitches. Even my fingertips begin to tingle with the new information. Her donor came from Texas. My brain is spinning a million miles a minute. Is this information useful? Sucking in a quick breath, I close out of her record and search up my own name and scroll back to my surgery. It takes me excruciatingly long seconds to find the information I need.

But there it is in black and white.

*Organ received in perfect condition from Texas.*

I sit back in the leather chair, stunned.

What are the odds Emily and I had our transplant on the same day and both our organs came from Texas? The logical conclusion would be that we got our organs from the same donor. I don't know that for sure, but I don't believe in coincidences. Sitting forward again, I run a search in the national hospital database. Any transplant surgery on that same day.

The cursor turns to an hourglass as it searches through the records. My foot begins to tap against the linoleum. I feel like I'm standing on the edge of a cliff, about to fall to my death with one click of the mouse. And then the screen changes and twenty-three records spit out. I pounce on the first one, desperate to find where the donor was from. Nope. That one was New Mexico.

The second record is where I hit pay dirt.

Ella Cooper, age twenty-seven, Arizona. Skin graft with donor from Texas.

I pull open a desk drawer and fumble around for a piece of paper and a pen, no longer able to go quietly. I scribble down her information and keep clicking, going through all twenty-three records until I have only six on my paper.

Me.

Emily MacDonald.

Ella Cooper.

Jack Murphy, fifty-three years old, New Mexico. Cornea transplant.

Toby Jackson, twenty-nine, paraplegic former military, California. Penile transplant.

Colin Davis, twenty-eight, Arizona. Bone graft.

The door bangs loudly against the love seat, jarring me from what I've learned. I gasp, grabbing my throat.

"Nicole?" Josephine's snippy voice only makes my heart race faster.

I click out of the database and reach below my knees to turn the computer off entirely. My hands are shaking so badly I can barely press the button. Josephine bangs the door against the love seat again.

"What are you doing? Open this door immediately!"

I jump to my feet and fold the paper with the six names, tucking it into the pocket of my slacks. "One second!" I call out, horrified when my voice shakes.

Breaking into patient medical records for personal gain is grounds for firing, and more than likely, legal action. Josephine is the last person who can catch me doing something I've never done before. She'll exploit it. Use it to hurt me.

I grab a picture frame out of my tote bag on my way over to the door. When I push the love seat away from the door, I have a pleasant smile on my face and a picture frame in hand.

Josephine is standing entirely too close to the door, her silk blouse perfectly pressed and her heels as sharp as the crease in her expensive trousers.

"Hey, Josephine. Did you come to help redecorate too?" I ask it loud enough that Helen can hear. "I rearranged the furniture, but I think I like it the way he originally had it."

Josephine narrows her eyes, her lips pinched into a disapproving frown. She looks behind me, but I keep my gaze steady on her face. I will not let this woman win.

"Are you okay?" I ask, feigning genuine concern. I lift my hand to touch her arm, but she jerks away from me.

"What are you doing here?" she spits at me, bony arms folding over her chest.

I blink. "I just told you. Is your hearing okay?"

I could swear Helen's cough from behind Josephine is actually muffled laughter. Josephine only scowls harder. She really is terrifying. It wouldn't surprise me one bit to find a trail of people she's stepped on over the years to find her way to the tippy top of Rosebud Grove society. Once I figure out this Emily situation, I'll find her skeletons. Mark my word.

She sniffs, lifting her nose in the air. "Where is Asher?"

"He's at a conference," Helen and I say at the same time.

Josephine doesn't like that. Me and Helen knowing something she doesn't sticks in her craw. Her arms drop and she pulls herself to her full height.

"You shouldn't be in his office. It's for authorized personnel only."

I grin. "I guess that means you shouldn't either."

Helen must be catching a cold with all the coughing she's doing as she types frantically on her computer, nails click-clacking away.

Josephine tilts her head to the side. "I'll walk you out, then."

I hold up the picture frame, the one with a photo from

our engagement session before my surgery. In it, he's smiling down at me like nothing on this planet matters more than me. "Let me put Asher's favorite photo on his desk, and then I'll be ready to leave."

Josephine waits for me, as if she's the hospital security rather than a measly board member. Helen rolls her eyes behind Josephine's back as we leave the office. It's only when we're out in the hallway and no one is around that Josephine drops the facade.

"I don't know what you think you're doing, but you better watch your step," she hisses.

I can practically feel the paper in my pocket burning a hole through the fabric. I don't need issues with Josephine distracting me from figuring out why Emily felt like talking to me was more important than checking herself into the hospital when it was clear she was dying.

"Have a beautiful day, Josephine." I smile at her, though it takes all my acting skills to make it happen. She harrumphs and walks off to spread her negativity elsewhere.

I watch her go until she turns the corner, then I take a steadying breath. I have to visit human resources to extend my medical leave before I go. They don't question me or make me jump through hoops. They just click a few buttons and tell me I'm good to go.

*Thank you, Kingsley connection.*

It's only as I'm rushing to my car in the parking garage that I have a strange feeling wash over me. I spin around, thinking someone is behind me, but no one's there. I scan the various cars parked nearby, but don't see anyone watching me from inside their cars. Shadows border every parked car. Since when did this parking garage get so dark?

I shake my head at myself and walk with steady steps to my SUV. I'm letting Emily's paranoia get to me. No one is after me except for Josephine, and I think she'd draw the line with attacking me in the parking garage. Too physical for her. She'd resort to emotional blackmail to put me in my place without bringing drama to the Kingsley name.

Even so, I look in my back seat before climbing into my vehicle and heading for home.

# CHAPTER TEN

"*D*arling?"

I jolt, Asher's voice pulling me out of the depths of the internet. I shut the laptop and stand, stretching away the tight muscles. It's gotten dark outside, as evidenced by the living room being cloaked in shadows. I should have turned a light on. I look down and realize I forgot to change into nicer clothes before Asher got home like I'd planned.

"Hey." I hurry over to his side and kiss his cheek. He pulls me close and then props his chin on the top of my head.

"Hey. Everything okay? I texted you to see if you wanted me to bring home some dinner." He thrusts a bouquet of red roses at me. "And I got you these, to celebrate your first week away of retirement."

My eyes widen. I wrap my hands around the gorgeous bouquet, feeling terrible. "I'm so sorry. I didn't see your text, and I forgot to start dinner. Are you hungry? I can make some sandwiches or something."

He smiles down at me, but I can see he's still worried. "It's fine. I brought home takeout. It's on the table."

Damn. I hadn't even heard him come in the door. My stomach growls loud enough for even our neighbors to hear. Asher slides his fingers through mine and tugs me toward the dining room. I can feel his gaze raking over me, trying to find answers to a question he's hesitating to ask. I grab a vase from the sideboard and put the flowers in it. After dinner, I'll fill it with water.

I pat his chest as he pulls out a chair for me. "I feel fine, by the way. I was just busy with wedding stuff."

It's a lie, but it rolls off my tongue easily. It's been my scapegoat for every moment lost in thought or hour spent on my laptop.

He kisses the top of my head and then has a seat to my right. White Styrofoam containers litter the dark wood table. He's bought enough food to feed an army. Maybe I'll remember to eat the leftovers for lunch tomorrow instead of fasting all day. That weight I've gained since my surgery is slowly starting to come off again. If I'm not careful, my wedding dress won't fit on our big day.

We dig in while he fills me in on his day. It's been a week since I logged into the hospital database and found out about the five other people who received an organ from Texas the same day I did. I've combed their social media accounts and come up with very little to explain why Emily felt threatened. I'm close to believing she was simply mentally insane.

"Mother asked where you were today. I think she misses seeing you around the hospital."

I blink away my thoughts. Asher's beautiful lips are tilted up in a smirk. I smile back, even though the mention of his mother sets my teeth on edge.

"I'm sure she does," I answer dryly.

In truth, it's been pleasant not having to go into the hospital. I've missed seeing Ruby, but avoiding Josephine has been an even nicer bonus. Honestly, I've forgotten all about her in my mad rush to find out about these other transplant patients.

Asher reaches over and holds my hand. "I know she's not the easiest woman to get along with, but she does want the best for us and the hospital. I'd like to see you two get along."

Where is this coming from? Asher has never asked me to get along with his mother. He knows I barely tolerate her. I tilt my head to the side, thoughts whirling. I suddenly have no appetite.

"Did she say something that makes you think we *don't* get along?"

Asher takes a moment before he answers, which I know means he's choosing his phrasing carefully. "No, not exactly. She's just worried about your frame of mind right now. She said you were acting strangely at the hospital last week and suggested we may want to postpone the wedding."

I rear back. "Postpone? No. Absolutely not, Asher."

He squeezes my hand again, leaning closer. "I know, darling. I know you want to get married as soon as possible, and so do I, but I will not ever compromise your health."

I push my chair back and stand. His hand falls off of mine. I break out into jumping jacks right there at our dining room table, probably looking like I've lost my mind. He stands too, holding his hands out like he wants to stop me.

"I'm fine!" I holler while still jumping. "I'm so tired of everyone walking on eggshells around me. Please don't be another person who thinks I can't stand up to the pressures of life, Asher!"

"Darling, please." Asher grabs me around the waist and carries me like a princess to the living room where he sits on the couch and cradles me in his lap. "Shhh."

My heart is thundering, but only in a way that reminds me I'm alive and should probably do more long walks in the morning to get in shape. Asher rubs my back with one big hand, his touch soothing in a way nothing else can. When I've caught my breath, I lift my head from where it's been tucked in the crook of his neck.

"I'm okay. I want to marry you in sixteen days. I'd marry you tonight in my scrubby sweatpants if you'd let me." Tears swim across my eyes.

Asher swipes away the first one to fall down my cheek. "Okay. I believe you. I was just so scared when you were getting worse and didn't have a match yet. I just kept wondering if you'd survive long enough so I could make you my wife." He tucks a lock of hair behind my ear. "I sometimes forget you're a tough nurse. You know your limits, and I need to trust your judgement. Forgive me?"

I throw my arms around his neck. "Of course I forgive you!"

It's not him I'm mad at. It's his damn mother. She's the one who put it in his head that I'm not fit to get married. I bet she'd love it if we postponed the wedding. Then she'd find a way for Asher to call the whole thing off.

I refuse to give her the satisfaction.

Asher runs his fingers through my hair and pulls my face to his. His kiss is passionate, the kind that says more than words ever could. When he picks me back up and carries me to our bedroom, I don't resist in the slightest. I have a wedding to attend in sixteen days, and I'm still hoping I'll be pregnant when I stand up there and say my vows. That'll show Josephine I'm not only fit to get married, I'm fit to carry Asher's child.

MUCH LATER, after Asher falls asleep with a lock of his golden hair falling over his eyebrows, I sneak out of bed and grab my laptop off the couch. The battery's almost dead, so I plug it into the outlet behind the couch and pull a blanket over my legs before plopping the laptop down too. There's a message waiting for me in the inbox of the email address I created just a few days ago.

This week has been eye opening in terms of the dark side of the internet. Every piece of information you could ever want is totally accessible. You just need to know how.

Or know some*one* who knows how.

Emily told me she was a computer hacker before she died. I was able to look up each and every person who commented on her social media over the last two years, zeroing in on two names. I reached out to both, expressing interest in finding buried information. The first never got back to me. But the second? His name is James Hill and he's in my inbox now, asking who I am and how I know Emily.

I don't lie to James. The man is potentially a genius computer hacker and could find out who I am very easily. I only know enough about IP addresses to know I'd get caught if I tried anything illegal. I write him back immediately.

*I met Emily the night she died. I believe she and I were the recipients of organs from the same donor. She had a terrifying message for me, and I'm trying to decipher it. Do you know anyone who could help me dig a bit deeper into donor records?*

Not two minutes after I hit send, James replies simply with a link. My finger hovers over it for a straight minute, thinking about the consequences. If I click it, I could be hacked. I could lose this computer, but then again, not much is on it. I could be exposed for asking my question, but honestly, I didn't ask anything horrible. Certainly nothing criminal.

Finally my finger drops on the trackpad and I click on the

link. My computer screen instantly goes black, and I have an awful feeling that I made a mistake. I'm about to move the computer off my lap in case it catches fire and deconstructs like a James Bond movie gone bad. I almost cackle out loud that my contact's name is James. How ironic.

Except that's when I notice a simple white cursor blinking in the top left corner. I squint and lean forward, only to jump back when words appear on the screen.

*Hope you didn't have anything on this computer you didn't want wiped. I think I can get you what you need. How much are you willing to pay?*

I sit back, heart thundering. Holy shit. I think I found a hacker to help me. But what's the going rate of computer hackers these days? Hundreds? Thousands? I begin to chew on my thumbnail. I can't mess this up. I really need James's help.

*I'm willing to pay well for you to access the national donor records and find out who the donor is. And to confirm there were only six of us that got organs. I need this information ASAP.*

I wait, chewing my nail again while I wait. James is a quick typer, thankfully.

*Five thousand, half now, half after. I'll get the info to you twenty-four hours after you pay the first half.*

I throw my hands in the air in a silent celebration. I click the link James sent with his message and wire over twenty-five hundred dollars. Once I get the confirmation of the money sent, James sends the thumbs up emoji and my screen goes black again.

Slamming the laptop shut, I lean back against the couch cushions, heart thundering as I think about the progress I've made here tonight. While it might be illegal to hack into the national records for donors, is it really that bad to want to know who saved my life?

I put the laptop aside and stand. My brain is buzzing with

possibilities, so I head for the kitchen for a glass of water before bed. A flash of light outside the kitchen window has me pressing against the wall and darting furtive looks out the window. Our kitchen faces our next-door neighbor, the one with the incessantly barking dog. Come to think of it, that dog hasn't made a peep since I gave it my pills.

I know I saw a light flash through our window. Could it have been someone with a flashlight? Someone trying to see in? I don't see anyone out there any longer, but it is almost midnight. If someone were dressed in black, I wouldn't be able to see them. Instead of getting water, I twist the blinds closed. Then I dash for the dining room and close the curtains. Now I'm in a panic, rushing around the house, making sure all the doors and windows are locked and the curtains are closed.

Standing in the middle of the living room, I force myself to take a deep breath and then let it out, nice and slow. I'm doing it again. I'm acting paranoid because a dying girl lost her mind in her last moments on this earth.

*Coming for all of us, Nicole Renee Kelly.*

Thanks for freaking me out, Emily. May you rest in more peace than you've given me.

ASHER DOESN'T FALL ASLEEP AS QUICKLY the following night, which has me on edge. I want to dash to my laptop and see if James has responded with the information I requested, but I can't do that until Asher is fast asleep.

"Come here, darling," Asher murmurs, pulling me into his chest, fitting himself behind me.

He's like a heat rock, cradling me in his embrace.

Normally this would be my favorite place to be. His hands run up and down my body, which feels like heaven. My eyelids get heavy, and before I know it, I'm asleep.

I wake with a jolt, Asher still wrapped around me. He's snoring softly in my ear. My heart's pounding, realizing I have to get to my laptop. The clock on my nightstand says it's just after one in the morning. I definitely should have a message from James by now. Lifting Asher's arm, I roll out from under him and get to my feet quietly. I grab my robe off the chair and wrap it around me.

My laptop takes forever to boot up to my normal desktop. I head straight for my email and see a new one from James. Inside of it is simply a link. I click it and the screen goes black again. While I wait, I start to chew on my thumbnail. I'm not sure when I picked up that habit, but it's oddly comforting.

The cursor appears and I hold my breath.

I don't even know what I'm hoping to learn, but I just can't dismiss the fact that Emily was legitimately scared about something. She came all that way to warn me. To warn me of what?

That's what I have to figure out.

*There are six of you who received organs or tissue from the same donor. His name is Cyrus Gene Bixler. I'd suggest not googling him. I wish I hadn't.*

And then he posts the link to pay him the second half of his fee. I memorize the name Cyrus Gene Bixler, then click on the link and take care of payment.

The screen flashes, the black screen gone and my normal desktop restored. With shaking hands, I hurry to open a web browser and type in the name of the man who saved my life.

The webpages that populate have my mouth dropping open.

Dread lines my gut.

I've gone down the rabbit hole and now I wish I was up in the sunlight, oblivious to what I've found.

Cyrus Gene Bixler lost his life at Three Rivers Correctional Facility in Texas. He was executed for his crimes.

Seventeen murders.

"Oh my God," I whisper to myself.

A serial killer's heart now beats in my chest.

And I'm not sure how I feel about it.

# CHAPTER ELEVEN

"You've gone quiet on me, darling," Asher says as he comes up behind me in the bathroom the next morning. He nuzzles into my neck while his arms steal around my waist. "Am I not giving you enough rest?" He wags his eyebrows in the mirror.

It's good to see him playful with me instead of concerned. "You've been perfect." I twist my neck and kiss him. It's rare that he's home this late in the morning, so I treasure these moments with him.

His hand drifts down to my thigh and under my robe. Just when my breath starts to come hot and heavy, he pulls back, regret painted across his face. "I have to go, sadly. I'm already late. How about I leave early today and take my future bride out to dinner?"

"I'd love that." I reach up on my toes to kiss him quickly. "Also, I want to talk to you about a health retreat in New Mexico I was thinking about going to. It's a last-minute thing, but I think it would be good for me, and I could see my dad again."

Asher cradles my cheek, nodding. "I think that sounds

amazing. You jumped right back into working after physical therapy released you. You should have more time to relax and rejuvenate."

He's so good to me. "I love you."

He grins and my heart flip-flops in my chest. "I love you too."

He leaves for work and takes all the light and goodness with him. When I hear the garage door rumble closed, I sag down onto the bed again. After finding out last night that the heart of a murderer beats in my chest, I felt a strong urge to see my father. He's as practical as they come. I know he'll be able to talk me down from my panic. It's not even really panic at this point.

I feel shame.

I feel dirty.

I also decided last night that I can't tell Asher about my donor. Besides the illegal nature of breaking into medical records, he was so excited when we got the news that they'd found me a heart. Our wedding is just over two weeks away. How does one bring up that a serial killer saved their life? Over a fancy dinner? Casually over coffee in the morning? There's not a good time to tell him, so I just won't. I love Asher, and this is my burden to bear. Not his. I'll take this little secret to my grave, which will hopefully be a long, long time from now.

The next morning, I kiss Asher goodbye and head for the airport in the ride share Asher ordered for me. Dad was all too happy for me to come visit again when I called him. The retreat doesn't begin until tomorrow, but that'll give me time to chat with Dad before it starts.

"Hey, pumpkin." My eyes squeeze shut at his familiar greeting when he picks me up from the airport. His hug is everything I need right now.

I wait until we get to his cozy but dilapidated house and

have lunch before I tell him everything I've found. The grilled cheese and heart pills go down the hatch and then I tell him. I don't go into how I got the information, but once I drop the bomb about the donor, he's distracted enough that he doesn't question me.

He scrubs an oil-stained hand across his beard, then settles back in his recliner chair. His hands fold over his belly and he begins to rock back and forth. This, too, is familiar. Dad always quietly mulls over things before speaking.

"I feel ashamed. I feel...a bit like the heart I have is somehow tainted."

He nods, then purses his lips. When he speaks, it's with authority and zero wiggle room. "The heart is just a pile of tissue, Nicole. Who you are as a person has nothing to do with that organ he gave you. That's like saying patients who receive titanium hips and knees are somehow no longer human. It's a ridiculous thought, right?"

I nod, seeing his point.

He leans forward, eyes bright. "You remain who you've always been. Finding out this information doesn't change that."

I lick my lips, feeling scared to give voice to the theories from some of the articles I read last night. "But there are some studies that say cells and tissue retain memory."

"Good thing you didn't get a brain transplant, then, huh?"

My lips hitch upward though nothing is actually funny about this situation. "No. They said I was too hardheaded for one of those."

Dad smiles, all the worry gone from his expression. "That's my girl!" He points to the remote lying on the coffee table in front of me. "Hand me the remote, will you? Now that we've solved your existential crisis, I think *Jeopardy* is on."

I huff a laugh. Dad and his *Jeopardy*. I hand him the

remote. He's not wrong though, I do feel a bit better just hearing him say my concerns are unfounded. Now that that's settled for now, I need to get to the real reason I flew out here to New Mexico. "Hey, do you mind if I take your truck out for a drive?"

The sounds of the television show swallow up the tiny space. "Sure, pumpkin. Just don't stay out late."

I roll my eyes, but he can't see me as I snatch the keys off the kitchen counter. "I'm not sixteen any longer, Dad."

"And thank God for that, huh?" He cackles, which turns into a session of wet hacking that has my nurse brain worried.

I head out once it subsides, shaking my head at how much I've come to appreciate the finer things in life. Dad's truck is so old school I have to roll down the window using elbow grease instead of pressing a button. I check the address on my phone, plugging it into my maps and following the route to the tiny town just south of Dad's place.

The neighborhood gets a little nicer the closer I get to my destination. Roads here have sidewalks and in-ground sprinklers. Homes are a little less dense and children leave bicycles on their front lawns without fear of them being stolen. My maps tell me I've arrived. I pull up to the curb and shut off the engine. I look up, wishing there were more streetlights around here. I'm completely in the dark, which might be good since I shouldn't really be here.

The house I'm looking for is a typical southwest home with an abundance of stucco and a red tile roof. A small patch of cut green grass tells me someone takes care of the place. I stay in the truck, observing from afar. Lights are on in several of the rooms facing the street, though the curtains are drawn. My thumb taps out a rhythm on the steering wheel. Should I knock? Or should I leave this alone?

I think about the warning Emily gave me before she died. I still haven't been able to figure out if any of that was valid or if she was just paranoid. Seems like a crappy thing to do to another transplant patient, make them wonder if someone is after them when you have no proof.

Resting my head back against the headrest, I sit there in the truck at the curb for a long time, just thinking about what it means to have the organs of a serial killer. Maybe it's best the others don't know. I think I might even nap for a bit right there on the side of the road. By the time I start the truck and head back to Dad's house, I have concluded that he's right.

This changes nothing.

And no one is after me.

I would know, wouldn't I?

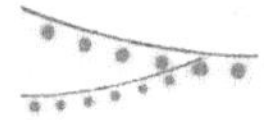

ASHER SURPRISES me by being the one to pick me up from the airport instead of one of the car companies he usually arranges. He's holding a bouquet of roses in my favorite deep red. I nearly crush them in my rush to give him a hug.

"Welcome home, darling," he murmurs, holding me tight. "You look refreshed."

I pull back to bury my nose in the blooms. "I *feel* refreshed."

And I do. After a bit of a rough start to my trip, the health retreat was just what I needed to clear my mind and relax my body. Asher takes care of getting my bag in the truck and we're off, back to the house.

"Dad showed me the tuxedo he plans to wear to our wedding."

Asher takes his gaze off the road for a moment to throw me a smile. "I bet he'll look amazing walking you down the aisle." He raises our joined hands and kisses the back of mine. "Then again, anyone would look amazing with your beauty on their arm."

I melt into my seat. "You are quite the charmer, Asher Kingsley."

He squeezes my hand but focuses on the road. "I'm just madly in love with you, Nicole Kelly."

His phone vibrates in the cup holder and the word "Mother" appears on his navigation screen. He hits a button on the steering wheel and the call goes away.

There goes all my good vibes.

I let a beat or two of silence go by before speaking. "Everything okay with your mother?"

Asher's jaw clenches. He turns into our neighborhood and slows down. "She's fine. Just pressing me to do another fundraiser. This time to benefit mental health services in Rosebud Grove. She's been going on about an increase in suicides nationally, but also one in particular that happened this week."

"Oh?" Josephine is always pressing Asher to do more than he possibly can. I really wish she'd get a hobby to occupy her time so Asher can be home more than he normally is.

"Yeah, it actually happened in New Mexico, not far from where your dad lives."

I frown, but Asher clicks the button to open the garage door and pulls his truck inside.

"I had dinner delivered while I was picking you up. Hope you're in the mood for pasta."

I'm actually starving. The food at the retreat was vegetarian, which I'd normally like, but lately I've been craving steak. An idea has my pulse hammering.

Could I be pregnant?

In all the craziness after Emily died on my doorstep, I haven't paid much attention to my cycle. I have to look at the period tracker app on my phone. With my attention now on a potential pregnancy, Asher and I eat dinner together, each talking about everything we've done since I've been gone.

Asher wipes his mouth with a napkin and tosses it down on the kitchen counter. "I have to leave tomorrow for that conference in Las Vegas. Should only be gone a couple days. Will you be lonely here by yourself?"

I slide off my barstool and onto his lap. "I'll miss you dreadfully, but I'll also call Ruby. Maybe she can stay with me. It'll be like a sleepover."

He kisses me, his hands kneading the flesh on my back. "I'll miss you dreadfully too."

After he drifts to sleep later that night, I sit up in bed and grab my phone off the bedside table. Keeping the screen as dark as I can, I order five pregnancy tests to be delivered to the house tomorrow. If I am pregnant, I plan to tell Asher on our wedding night. My wedding gift to him will be a son or daughter who will hopefully look just like him.

When that's done, I start chewing on my thumbnail, tossing looks at Asher. Throwing caution to the wind, I enter a search about a recent suicide in New Mexico.

There it is, in the same small town I drove to. Warning bells begin to clang in my head. My nose goes numb but I press on, clicking on the first article that was updated just tonight.

*Jack Murphy, a 53-year-old man from Glorieta, New Mexico, was found deceased at his home by a concerned niece who came by to check on him early Tuesday morning. A knife wound to the throat was the official cause of death, not a typical way to end one's life, but with a suicide note found next to the body, officials have indicated no foul play. "He'd just gotten a cornea transplant last year," his niece tells* The Santa Fe Times. *"He was doing so well. Only recently he began to complain of some eyesight issues. I had no idea it had gotten this bad."*

My hands are shaking so badly I can't read the rest of the article. I slide out of bed and walk as quickly and quietly as I can to the living room. Tears flood my eyes, making it impossible to read the rest of the article.

*There must be some mistake.*

I get down on my hands and knees to retrieve the piece of paper I stashed under the couch where I knew Asher would never look. My handwriting is barely legible in the darkness. I have to turn on a lamp before I can verify that indeed, Jack Murphy, was one of the organ recipients on my list.

Six of us who received an organ from the Texas serial killer.

Two of them are now dead.

One died on my doorstep.

And I was sitting outside Jack Murphy's house the night before he was found dead. I wonder if I'd knocked on his door if I could have stopped him.

"Oh fuck," I manage to say before I get lightheaded and have to bend over at the waist to put my head between my knees.

# CHAPTER TWELVE

To say I've become paranoid is an understatement.

Asher is already gone when I wake up the next morning after a fitful night staring up at the ceiling with a spinning brain, interspersed with nightmares when I did manage to catch some sleep.

Every curtain is drawn. Every door is locked. I checked. Twice.

I feel safe within these four walls.

Sadly, I have a life to live, which requires stepping foot outside. I curse under my breath, knowing I'll be late for my final dress fitting if I don't get going. I know I look as exhausted as I feel when I reach the dress shop. The French woman who owns the place frowns the second she sees me. Instead of champagne, she offers me coffee, which I appreciate, even if it's a bit of a backhanded gesture. She ends up having to take in the waist just a bit, chiding me for losing weight when I've worked so hard to gain it after the surgery. I promise to eat more and turn to leave.

Someone in a coat vanishes around the corner of the store, just a flash of dark material through the window. It could be nothing, but something about it has my senses on high alert.

"Are you okay, my dear?" the owner asks me, peering out the window in the same direction I'm staring. Her arms are full of the white lace and satin that is my wedding gown.

I force a smile on my face, even though my limbs have begun to shake. "Yes. I just thought I saw someone."

The woman studies me, then snaps her fingers over her head. Another woman rushes out from behind a curtain to stand next to her. "You will walk Ms. Kelly to her car."

I start to protest, then rethink it. It would be nice to be walked out to my car. The woman dutifully walks me out, her accent not as thick as the owner's. She's kind, waits for me to get in my car and lock the door before she steps back. When I pull away from the curb, she's still there, watching me.

"Pull your shit together, Nicole," I mutter to myself. There's no sign of anyone in a dark overcoat on the sidewalk in downtown Rosebud Grove.

My phone rings, making me nearly slam on my brakes. As it is, a car behind me honks and zooms around me in the other lane. I answer the call through the Bluetooth and try to focus on my speed.

"You doing okay with Asher gone?" Ruby asks by way of greeting.

It shouldn't surprise me she knows Asher's schedule. She's been a good friend, checking in on me constantly for years now.

"Yeah."

There must be something in my tone because she doesn't waste much time doing what my best friend always does. "Uh-huh. Sure. Hey, how about I come over tonight? We can have a good ol'-fashioned sleepover."

Relief floods through me, tamping down some of the

paranoia. "Yeah, that sounds great. I'll order in food from Roberto's."

"Make it fattening as hell and I'm in."

We confirm plans and then she hangs up. When I get home, I'm sure to pull into the garage, lower the garage door, and then get out, my cell phone in hand in case I need to call 911. So much for thinking the paranoia had lessened. I spend the rest of the day doing more research in comfortable sweats.

By the time Ruby comes over in the beat-up silver Camry that I tease her isn't nice enough to drive through this neighborhood, I've convinced myself that Emily was on the right track. She knew what was going on before me. I should try to contact the rest of the organ recipients to warn them that someone is trying to kill us all. I know it sounds crazy, but what are the odds that two out of the six recipients are dead?

"Hey, gorgeous!" Ruby shouts in my ear as I let her in and she swoops me up in a hug. "I brought light beer!"

The doorbell rings before she's even gotten her coat off. "That should be the food." I purposely had it scheduled to be delivered after Ruby was already here for safety's sake. I swing open the door and release a breath once I see that it's a legit food delivery service, not someone here to kill me.

We get settled on the floor of the living room, food and beer in hand. Ruby tells me the latest gossip from the hospital. She's so vibrant, so alive, it makes me jealous. I wonder if I've ever been that lighthearted. That excited about life without a worry like impending death hanging over my head. Before I got my heart, I felt that constant pressure of looming death. Now, even after my surgery, I fear for my life.

"Okay." Ruby clinks her empty beer bottle down on the coffee table. "What's going on with you, girl? Shouldn't you be high on bridal plans and riding off into the sunset with your doctor fiancé?"

Her kind dark eyes beg me to confide in her. If there's one person who will believe me, it's Ruby. Asher would probably brush aside my paranoia in an attempt to make me feel better in the moment, but not Ruby. So I tell her.

Almost everything.

An anonymous organ donor from Texas. The recipients. The two who've now died.

By the time I'm done, she's shell-shocked, eyes wide with either shock or horror. Or maybe both. Imagine if I told her the organ donor was a serial killer? That's a secret I'll take to my grave.

I hand her another beer out of the six-pack she brought. She twists off the top and takes a long sip before she speaks. She plops the bottle down on the coffee table and crawls closer to grab my hands.

"Nicole. Listen to me. You have to drop this. Walk away from all this crap that's stressing you out. The doctor told you Emily was already dying. Her body was actively rejecting those lungs. This Jack guy could have been suicidal for years before his surgery. The two are ninety-nine percent unrelated. You're working yourself up over nothing when you should be focused on your wedding."

Well, I guess maybe even Ruby doesn't believe me. "I wish I could drop it, Rubes. But there's something in me telling me there's more to the story here."

"Have you told Asher all this? What does he say?" Ruby takes another swig of her beer.

I shake my head, looking down at where I've been picking at my thumbnail. The damn thing has started to bleed. "No. I haven't said anything to Asher. And I don't want you to either."

Ruby looks at me like I'm an unruly child. "I think you should tell him."

"Well, I don't. I told you all that in confidence, Ruby."

She holds her hands up. "Okay, okay. I won't say anything, but for the record, I vote for telling Asher."

We agree to disagree and start up a movie. By the time it's over, Ruby is asleep on the couch and I'm scrolling on my phone, looking up the other organ recipients. Toby Jackson lives in northern California, only a two-hour drive from here. I watch Ruby sleep, thinking the smart thing to do would be to take her advice and let this whole thing drop.

But there's a big part of me that knows something's going on. My faulty heart has directed my life for more years than I'd like to admit. Now that I have a new one, I don't want to passively sit back and see what happens. I want to create my own fate. I want to face this phantom head-on.

So I message Toby Jackson on his one and only social media account that I could find, letting him know who I am and that I'd like to come speak to him.

It's not until the early hours of the next morning that he answers me back.

*I don't know how you got my name, but what the hell. Come on by.*

WITH ASHER OUT of town and Ruby working long shifts at the hospital, I have time to drive south the next day, all the way to Toby Jackson's house in Yreka. The neighborhood doesn't look all that safe, but then again, everywhere has been feeling dangerous, even Rosebud Grove. I scan the street before climbing out of my car. When it looks clear, I lock my car and hustle to Toby's front door. My fist raps on the door once, then twice.

I hear his voice, saying to calm down.

Then the door swings open. I have to look down to see Toby Jackson. He's in a wheelchair. No legs. In all the rush to talk to one of the recipients, I didn't do my research well enough to know Toby's injuries.

"Hi. I'm Nicole Kelly," I say after a moment of hesitation.

He holds out his hand, and I shake it. He rolls his chair back and I follow him inside his dark house, closing the door behind us and locking it. While he wheels into another room, I follow, taking in his home. It's decorated nicely, as if a woman's touch had been here at one time, but stacks of dirty dishes and clothes line every surface.

"Excuse the mess," Toby says as he stops in the living room. He points to a couch, where I have to push a laundry basket to the side in order to sit. "Ella used to be the one who did the housework."

I tilt my head to the side. "Ella?"

Toby's face, haggard and unshaved, is pinched when he answers. "Ella Cooper. My fiancée. Well, former fiancée. We broke up a month ago."

"I'm sorry to hear that." I mean it too. I'd be heartbroken to lose Asher. But I can't seem to focus on that when her name rings a bell.

Ella Cooper.

She was one of the names on my list. Six recipients. Ella is one of them.

"She was an organ recipient too," Toby is saying.

"How...?" I'm baffled, too stunned to form a coherent sentence.

Toby huffs. "We met at the hospital. Recovered together and fell in love."

"Do you mind if I ask what happened?"

Toby begins to get agitated, rolling his chair back and forth a few inches, as if he can't keep his hands still. His face goes through several expressions, only to land on what can be described as rage. His skin turns a purplish red that spells trouble. I sit up taller, wondering if I can outrun him to the front door if I need to. Warning bells clang in my brain. I'm an idiot for coming here without telling anyone where I am. Or bringing a weapon of some sort.

"Listen. I was in the army." Toby lets go of the wheelchair long enough to scrape a hand down his face. He looks much older than the twenty-nine years listed in his medical records. "Lost my legs in a car bomb. Lost the use of some other things."

He mumbles the last part, and I nod to let him know I understand. Toby Jackson had a penile transplant, a controversial procedure without a great success rate. He's not the only soldier who's signed up for the surgery though. Medicine has been working hard to help the men and women who serve our country and pay the ultimate price. Loss of sexual function on top of whole limbs can cause many soldiers to slide into depression and suicidal thoughts. Helping them gain back some level of function is paramount for healthy longevity.

"Things were good," he finally says, tears filling his eyes. "I healed really well. We planned to get married." His voice crumbles.

I look away, giving him time to collect himself. When he does, his voice is a weird kind of disconnected. Like he's telling a story about himself he can't quite believe either.

"I began having some issues." He shrugs and then grips the armrests of his wheelchair so hard his knuckles turn white. "I don't know if it was the medication or something, but suddenly I couldn't control it."

I frown, lost. "Control it?"

"The urges!" he shouts, spit flying out of his mouth.

I jolt, muscles tight and ready to run.

"I went from disabled to having this...this...organ that I

couldn't control. I wanted to fuck everything that moved! I couldn't sleep, I thought about it so much. Do you know what it's like to have a hard-on for twenty-four hours straight? Sometimes days at a time?"

I don't answer, but I'm pretty sure he doesn't expect me to.

"Ella had to fight me off. I was ashamed of myself, forcing myself onto her at all hours of the day. And then any woman I saw became fair game. I was at the goddamn grocery store hitting on a lady twice my age. What the actual fuck? I was willing to cheat on Ella just to sate that fucking urge. It was like I got the transplant but lost my brain. I couldn't control myself!"

He's weeping now, all traces of anger gone in an instant. I swallow hard. The man is distraught. Clearly having issues with his organ transplant.

"I'm sorry she left you," I say quietly. His sobs intensify.

"I broke up with *her*." He raises his face from his hands. That horrible purple color is creeping back into his face. "I couldn't let her get hurt. Couldn't chance what I would do to her."

A chill runs up my back.

"What I could do to anyone."

Suddenly Toby's not crying any longer, though tears still stain his cheeks. He's staring at me like he's seeing me for the first time. I jump to my feet, manners completely forgotten. I'm listening to my instincts and my gut is telling me to get the hell out of here.

So I run.

His hand reaches for me as I dart past, snatching the hem of my blouse. My heart is pounding so loudly I can't hear my own scream. I lurch back when he tugs hard. In the scramble to get away, I lose my footing. I feel my body going down, but then it all goes black.

The next thing I know, I'm blinking my eyes open to find myself on the ground. I hear nothing. See no one. Just Toby Jackson's dirty kitchen floor against my cheek. Snippets of his story race through my brain and I scramble to my feet. I don't waste time looking for him or figuring out what happened. Survival instincts tell me to do one thing.

Run.

So I do.

# CHAPTER THIRTEEN

I race for the bathroom and empty the meager contents of my stomach. A light sheen of sweat takes over my skin, cooling off the hot wave of nausea. I flush the toilet, wipe my mouth, and sit back on the floor of our bathroom. A single tear slides down my cheek. There's a bruise on my arm. One I don't remember getting. Then again, I passed out at that guy's house. Hit the floor pretty hard.

I haven't been sleeping since I drove back from Yreka.

Visions of Toby Jackson's angry face and empty eyes haunt me whenever I try to rest. Ruby has stayed with me the last few days, sleeping in my bed and keeping me company. I have a feeling I would have crawled right out of my skin without her calming presence. She left for work this morning and took her duffle bag of belongings. Asher's flight lands in just a few hours and Ruby has a shift at the hospital. Surely I can keep my shit together for a few hours until Asher is back.

Still sitting on the floor, I open the cabinet to get more toilet paper and see the pregnancy tests I stashed there earlier this week.

"No time like the present," I tell myself out loud.

My stomach is still uneasy, but I'm able to get to my feet and open the first test. I follow the directions and pee on the stick, setting it on the counter afterward to wait exactly three minutes. The seconds tick by with agonizing slowness.

My feelings are all over the place.

I want to be pregnant. I want to start making a family with Asher more than anything. But I also am terrified someone is out to kill me for having the heart of a serial killer. And wouldn't being pregnant now be the worst timing ever? Could one of the serial killer's victims' family be after us? Maybe the serial killer had mentally ill friends who are hunting us for sport? Nothing makes sense, but the terror I feel is very real.

The timer on my phone goes off and my fingers tremble as I pick up the test. Closing my eyes, I say a prayer for... something. Just help, I guess. I need help to deal with my life, and either way this test goes, I'll need help to absorb the news. I can't even share this moment with Asher. He has no idea I've gone off birth control. I just didn't want to hear his daily concern about my health. My doctor said I'm strong enough to get pregnant, and that's the energy I want to take into a possible pregnancy.

On the count of three, I flip the test over. My knees give out and I sink back down to the floor. Sobs burst out of me, loud and echoing in the cavernous tile bathroom.

It's positive.

I'm pregnant.

Three hours later, I'm dressed, hair curled, makeup on, and drops in my eyes to cover the redness. Asher comes walking through the garage door, suitcase in hand.

"Hey, darling." His lopsided smile and soothing voice are everything I need in this moment.

I go to him, sinking into his embrace as he puts down the

suitcase and laying my head on his chest. The steady beat of his heart is a metronome of calm.

"Hey," I whisper back.

He pulls out of the hug too soon for me, but puts his hands on my arms. "What do you say I play hooky the rest of the day and we snuggle on the couch to watch a movie?"

I'm instantly happier, mood lifted. "I say yes. I'll even let you pick the movie."

He laughs, wrapping his arm around me while we walk to our bedroom. "Let me get into something more comfortable."

He changes and I watch him, mesmerized by the fact that he's about to be a father. He'll be a good one. The best, actually. Sure, he works a lot, but he always makes me feel like a priority, and I know he'll do the same for our child. All that fear I've been living with the last few days slides away. There's no way anything will harm what he and I have. I'm letting the delusions of some mentally and physically ill people make me afraid.

Now more than ever, I can't tell Asher about my organ donor. I don't want him to worry that the mother of his child is carrying around the heart of a murderer. It'll be my secret, 'til the day I die. No one will ever know.

I'm also going to keep the pregnancy a secret. Just until our wedding night. I already searched online for the perfect gift to announce it to him.

Asher pulls me up from the chair, dressed in my favorite T-shirt. It's the softest thing he owns and he knows I can't keep my hands off him when he wears it. He shoots me a wink as we walk to the living room, and I don't think I've ever been happier than I am in this exact moment.

He tucks me into the couch with a blanket, then switches on the television. Handing me the remote, he heads for the kitchen to grab a bag of chips.

"I know you said I can pick, but I think you should. You know I'll just rewatch *Braveheart* and that'll bore you to tears," he calls from the kitchen.

He's not wrong. I think I've sat through at least ten showings of that movie, knowing it's his favorite. I start to flip through the channels menu while the news is playing in the background. No HGTV, though I'd love to watch a remodel to get decorating ideas for the nursery I'll get started on after the wedding.

"A man was found dead this morning in his Yreka home by his ex-fiancée. The incident has been declared an accident. He was a decorated military veteran with a Purple Heart for his bravery. It's been reported that he saved a soldier by staunching blood flow with his shirt despite his own catastrophic injuries that led to a double amputation a month later."

My finger freezes on the remote. The newscaster keeps talking, but I'm focused on the little square by his head that shows a picture of the man who died.

He's got tightly cut brown hair and brown eyes. It's obviously a much younger photograph from his military days, but there's no doubt it's Toby Jackson.

Nausea bubbles up, and I have to clap a hand to my mouth to keep from crying out in shock. I manage to turn up the volume and catch the end of the segment.

"Investigators have concluded that Mr. Jackson fell out of his wheelchair and hit his head, leading to a brain bleed. Living alone, he unfortunately wasn't found soon enough. Services will be held next week at Yreka Veterans Cemetery."

I press the mute button and drop the remote on the couch. All that worry and paranoia from earlier this week is back. Six recipients. Three are now dead.

And I've had contact in one way or another with all three.

What are the odds?

And what the hell happened two days ago in Toby's house? There's a black hole in my memory, taunting me.

"I've got one bowl of spicy nacho and one bowl of sea salt." Asher comes back in the room carrying two bowls of chips, oblivious to the news report. He halts three feet from me, sensing something's off. "What's wrong?"

I try to paste on a smile, but I can feel how brittle it is. He has a seat next to me and puts the bowls on the coffee table. He grabs my icy cold hands and turns me to face him.

"Nicole, darling, talk to me. What just happened?"

I swallow hard, wondering how much I can tell him. I feel like this has gotten way too big to not share. I can't tell him everything, but maybe parts of it would be okay?

I have to clear my throat for my voice to work. "So you know how that girl died on our doorstep?" He nods and I continue. "And then that guy died in New Mexico?" He frowns.

"He was a cornea transplant. Remember you said your mother wanted to focus a fundraiser on mental health because of it?"

Understanding dawns. "Yes, I remember now."

"And the news tonight just said a man died in Yreka. Another organ recipient. Don't you find that odd?"

Asher's eyes track back and forth on mine, searching for something. "I...don't understand. You and I both know organ donation is a very risky thing, even with all of our medical advancements. Those that come through the operation and recovery also have a lot of mental and emotional work to do. Sadly, not everyone can handle it. That's why you doing so well with your heart is truly a miracle." He squeezes my hands. "Don't go looking at the statistics, darling. Focus on your own recovery."

I open my mouth, but close it again. I can't tell him the three deaths are related without telling him I broke into confidential medical records. That's a felony. The future wife of the chief of staff can't be caught tampering with patient files. It would be the type of scandal that would ruin his career and force us to move from Rosebud Grove in disgrace.

I nod instead, not at all mollified. Asher smiles, but he's still searching my face.

"I think I'll talk with your doctors tomorrow. Run through your list of medications and latest blood draw. Make sure you're reacting correctly to the cocktail they have you on. Okay?" He sits back and wraps his arm around my shoulders. "You're okay. You're safe and healthy. I won't let anything happen to you."

We sit like that for several minutes while I try to calm my breathing. I can't tell Asher anything further or he'll make good on his promise to talk to my doctor. I can't have him asking questions and spoiling the surprise that I quit taking my birth control. But Asher's so very wrong. Nothing is okay. I'm not safe. And he can't stop what's happening.

Only I can.

Asher looks for the remote and finds it between the cushions. He teases me about not choosing something before he can select *Braveheart*, but I don't have the brain power to tease back. He presses play, settles into the couch with me tucked into his side, and crunches on the chips like everything is fine.

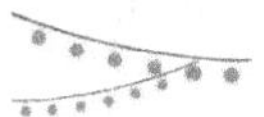

DESPERATE TIMES CALL for desperate measures. I've contacted my dark web person and hired him again to do a deep dive on the organ donor. I want to know everything about the man, his crimes, who he's wronged, and who are his friends and relatives. Did he have other victims that weren't tied to him in the court system? Someone who wanted revenge and didn't get it?

I've sharpened my own investigative skills too. I've reached out to Jack Murphy's family for more information on his last days and frame of mind. I've also reached out to Emily MacDonald's parents to see if they have any insight on what she was trying to warn me about and why.

The last two remaining organ recipients have my full attention. Colin Davis remains a bit of a mystery. He lives in Arizona but has no social media. Ella Cooper is my next target. She's Toby's Jackson's ex-fiancée, a little twist I wasn't expecting that day I chatted with him. I have a feeling she'll be at his funeral, which is where I'm headed now.

It's a dark and dreary day for a funeral, though I guess any day would be rough to bury someone you love. I watch mourners surround the gravesite at Yreka Veterans Cemetery and choose to hang back on the periphery of the group. The minister gives a message meant to lift spirits and bless the dearly departed. I notice several other veterans in full military dress, saluting during the playing of Taps.

A tall blonde woman in a solid black suit tailored to perfection steps up at the end to take the urn from the table by the minister and put it into the ground. She tosses a white rose on top, swipes at her cheeks, and then moves aside. An older woman does the same, though her weeping can be heard from over here. I wait until everyone has disbursed and the groundskeepers arrive to finish the job of burying his remains.

The blonde woman shakes hands with almost everyone. When the funeral has cleared out and the woman gives the grave one last look, I approach. She's headed for her car.

"Hello, Ella, is it?"

She looks at me, light eyes swollen from crying but still

exquisitely beautiful. From the brief moments I spoke to Toby Jackson, Ella seems way out of his league. Then again opposites attract, and I'm all too aware that many think Asher is out of my league too. Love doesn't always make sense on paper.

"Yes. And you are?" Her voice is soft, hesitant.

I hold out my hand and she shakes it. I notice her wrist and hand is mottled with pink, healing skin. "I'm Nicole Kelly. A fellow organ recipient."

She tilts her head to the side, clearly confused. I rush on, hoping to get information from her about who might have been after Toby, or at the very least, warn her to watch her back.

"I've been doing some research, and I feel like there are quite a few of us having issues after we received organs." Again, I have to tread lightly. I can't tell her I hacked into the system and found out these organs were all from the same donor.

"What do you mean?"

I lick my lips, glancing around the cemetery. Everyone has cleared out, including the groundskeepers. "Did Toby mention any issues after he healed from his surgery?"

Ella's face goes pale. She swallows hard and gives me the barest of head nods to continue.

"Something's not right and I'm not sure if I'm being paranoid or if there really is someone stalking organ recipients."

Ella's hand flies to her throat. "Stalking?"

I wave my hand in the air between us. "I don't know. It's just a theory. Maybe this is all just regular side effects from receiving organ transplants. Again, I don't know. Are you recovering okay?" I nod my head toward her hand.

She covers the scars peeking out from her suitcoat with her other hand. When she speaks, I can barely hear her.

"The skin has been burning lately. The transplant doctor

assures me everything's fine though. I'm getting a second opinion when I move to Washington next week."

I frown, heart pounding. I can feel that I'm onto something. "And Toby?"

Ella's eyes fill with tears. "He was fine," she snaps.

I know that's not true. He told me that himself. He was having sexual urges he couldn't control. He literally said he felt like his brain was highjacked.

"Maybe he wasn't," I offer softly.

Ella drops her hands. "You're crazy. You know that? My fiancé just died and you come here to his funeral with insane accusations?" She spins to grab the door handle of her car. "You're fucking crazy, lady."

And with that, she's in her black SUV with a Hawaiian Islands sticker on the back, speeding out of the cemetery. I sigh and watch her drive away. I can imagine a woman wouldn't want to remember her fiancé as a guy who started having dreams of raping women.

It looks like Ella Cooper is a dead end.

# CHAPTER FOURTEEN

*I* wake midmorning to a note and a single red rose resting on Asher's pillow. All the note says is "one week." I smile, allowing myself to stay in that feeling you get first thing in the morning when all your worries are far away and anything seems possible.

One week until our wedding.

One week until I'm Mrs. Asher Kingsley.

I sit up slowly, letting my stomach get used to being upright before I get out of bed. I've noticed that any morning sickness tends to be held at bay if I move slowly and deliberately. Also, if I stay calm. Which I haven't been doing very often lately. Fear and anxiety have plagued me since discovering all the organ recipients have been dying.

Reaching for my cell phone on the bedside table, I push my hair out of my face and scan my email inbox. I stop on an email from a woman I don't know. Jasmine Ritter. The name doesn't ring a bell, but I click on it anyway.

My heart rate kicks up as I realize that Jasmine is Jack Murphy's niece, the one who found him dead in his house. I'd reached out to her to find any information I could on his suicide. Had he been suicidal beforehand? Was his recovery from the cornea transplant not going well? I hadn't expected to hear back from her, being that I'm a virtual stranger, but I had to try. Thankfully, she's chosen to be open and transparent.

*I'm not sure how much I can help. Uncle Jack was a quiet man. Didn't share much, but I was under the impression his transplant recovery had been going well. He's never had mental health issues before the accident either. It was a fluke fishing accident that caused him to lose his sight. His vision dimmed and then he lost all sight eventually. He never seemed upset about it, just took it in stride, which is why his suicide is so hard to understand.*

*After I got your email, I talked to my dad, who probably knew Uncle Jack best. He'd been having nightmares recently apparently. Seeing really grotesque scenes in his dreams. He laughingly told my dad that he had to stop watching horror movies and go back to Westerns.*

*I'm sorry I can't help more. If you find out anything, please let me know. I know the police ruled it a suicide, but that doesn't sit right in my gut. I've attached a photo of his suicide note. I'd appreciate it if you didn't share that with anyone.*

I click on the attachment and pull up a photo of a piece of paper. It's not a letter or anything like that. It's more like a diary entry. Jack doesn't address it to anyone. He just confesses to having troubling visions. Blood and gore and bodies of faceless people disturb his sleep. He even mentions calling his doctor to check on all his medications.

I put down my phone and climb out of bed. That doesn't read like a suicide note. A man who plans on taking his life doesn't discuss calling his doctor the next day, does he? I'm no closer to figuring this all out.

Frustrated, I get ready for the day, forcing myself to do my hair and makeup, and to get dressed. I can't live in fear, constantly looking over my shoulder. Taking time off from work was a good move on my part. At least now, I can hide out here in my house instead of having to see Josephine all the time at the hospital. One less thing to worry about as I mentally prepare for the wedding.

I spend the day doing more sleuthing online. My hacker contact, James, said he'll have a full report on the organ donor by tomorrow. Asher is late that evening, which isn't unusual. I track his phone, seeing that he's still at the hospital. I text Ruby, but she doesn't text back, which is not unusual either. She works long hours too.

My phone pings with an incoming message as I'm making dinner, a healthy chicken and vegetable stir-fry. I pick up the phone, hoping it's either Asher or Ruby, but it's Josephine. I drop the phone like it's a snake about to bite me.

So much for the peace of not having to see her. I grab one of Asher's beers out of the fridge and crack it open. I need reinforcements to deal with that woman. Just a couple sips. With a long pull of the craft IPA soaking into my bloodstream, I open the text and nearly choke. She's sent me a picture of her dress fitting.

*Josephine: Mother of the Groom dress fits perfectly. What do you think?*

She's covered head to toe in lace, which would normally be very pretty, but the color is a light cream. Almost white.

Like a bride.

Knowing screenshots are forever, I don't write back what I'd like to. Instead, I take the high road, knowing full well hell will freeze over before I let her wear that to my wedding.

*Me: I think something in a different color would suit your skin tone better.*

*Josephine: I think this'll do just fine.*

I want to throw my phone through the kitchen window. I'm so worked up, the chicken burns on the stovetop before I realize what's happening. I shut off the stove and throw the whole thing in the sink. I pace the house until I wear myself out. Sagging onto the couch, I grab a blanket and curl up, my head on a pillow. Getting to marry Asher is worth it, but sometimes I wonder why I have to fight so hard. Can't one thing in my life be simple? I begin to drift off as the sun goes down.

I dream of Josephine's face turning purple as my hands close around her skinny throat. Her eyes are wide with fear. She tries to scratch me with her claws, but she's no match for me. A rush of adrenaline has me feeling like I might be the strongest woman on the planet as the life drains out of her. When she slumps over, I let her body drop to the ground, an undignified heap. And then I begin to kick her, the crunch of bones like music to my ears.

"Nicole, darling." Asher shakes me awake.

I have to blink repeatedly to clear the images from my eyes. Damn.

"You're crying," he says softly, swiping his thumbs across my cheeks. "What's wrong? Are you still worried about those organ recipients?"

My gaze was locked on his, but now it flies past his shoulder to where Ruby appears. What's she doing here tonight? She winces at Asher's words. Instantly, I know what she's done.

I sit upright, pushing Asher's hands away from me. Nausea batters against my senses but I push it down. I don't have time for that right now.

"You told him?" I jump to my feet and square up with Ruby.

She won't hold my gaze. I bump her chest, then thump her on the shoulder. Her gaze flies to mine, startled.

"Look at me when you betray me, huh?" I shout.

"I d-didn't!" she stutters back, retreating a step. "I told

him you're very worried about those organ recipients and he needs to talk to you about it."

I tilt my head. "That's all, huh?"

Ruby looks me right in the eyes. "That's all."

She's a fucking liar.

"Nicole, darling." Asher grabs my hand and pulls me back to the couch. "It's okay. Please calm down. I just want to help you. So does Ruby. If you're worried, we're worried, okay?"

I glare at Ruby for a beat more before turning to Asher. "Yes, I'm still worried, but I'll be fine."

Asher looks at our entwined hands and frowns. He holds up my right hand. "What happened to your thumb?"

I snatch my hand back, knowing the skin around my thumb is bloody. "Nothing! I just cut myself cooking."

"You've never chewed your nails before," Asher murmurs, looking at me like I'm a bomb about to explode. Maybe he's right. I do feel like all the pressure lately is getting to me.

"I'm fine," I snap.

My tone, one I never usually use with him, just has the frown lines deepening.

Ruby steps closer, putting her hand on Asher's shoulder. "We want to help, Nicole. We're on your side."

I ignore her and look at Asher, anger bubbling hot and bright. He's the only one I totally trust at this point and even that trust is looking a bit flimsy. "What did Ruby say to you that got you worried?"

Asher goes to look up at Ruby and I tug his hand. "Don't look at her. Answer me."

His eyes widen at my tone, but he obliges. "She said you're very concerned about these dying organ recipients and there may be something to it. Said I needed to talk to you."

I jump to my feet and direct my ire at Ruby. "Is that why my fiancé is late? You cornered him after work and betrayed my trust? After I explicitly asked you to keep things between us? Or was he late because you were cornering him for other things? You look awfully cozy."

I look pointedly at her hand on his shoulder.

She snatches her hand back, her normally dark face now pale. "I know you're upset, but watch what you're saying. I would *never* betray your trust. You know that. I was your friend before I was his."

My thumb is between my teeth before I know I'm doing it. Pain blooms right as I taste something metallic in my mouth. It only makes me angrier.

I jab my finger in the middle of her chest. She gasps but I shout right over it. "I trusted you with my worries, and the first chance you got, you went and blabbed it to Asher! Some friend you are!"

Asher's arm bands around my waist and pulls me back from Ruby. He doesn't let go until the couch is between us and her.

"Hey," he whispers in my ear. "Nothing is going on with me and Ruby. I give you my word. But I *am* worried. Let's all sit and hash this out. Will you do that?"

I point at Ruby who looks like she's about to cry. "I'll hash it out with you, but she has to leave."

Asher nods over my head, and Ruby's gaze darts between the two of us. She must realize I mean business because she wipes a tear from her cheek and nods, then grabs her coat off the chair.

"I'm only trying to help you, Nicole," she says softly as she walks out. "Call me when you realize that."

We wait to hear the front door click shut. Asher spins me around and cups my face. "Sweetheart. Let's talk. Tell me everything bothering you. I promise to take it seriously. We're in this together. Always. Forever."

My eyes fill with tears. I need one person to be on my side. One person who won't betray me. If Ruby's coming after my fiancé, I won't let her. He's mine, and I won't let him go without a fight.

"Okay," I whisper back.

"Okay." He smiles, but it doesn't reach his eyes. "Have a seat and I'll go get us a drink."

I have my legs curled underneath me and the blanket over my lap when he comes back in with two crystal glasses filled with whiskey. He took his suit jacket and tie off  too.

He hands me a glass. "Here you go."

I lift an eyebrow, already much calmer with Ruby gone. "You're giving me alcohol to drink? Who are you and where did you put my fiancé?"

His lopsided grin is back. "Figured we could break a few rules tonight."

I snuggle in close to him. "I can agree to that." I take a sip and start to tell him about Toby Jackson and Ella Cooper. I leave out the shared organ donor. By the time I'm done explaining, I've drained my glass and I'm so tired I can't seem to keep my eyes open.

Asher stands, putting down his full glass and lifting me into his arms. "Come to bed, darling."

My head feels like it weighs a hundred pounds. It's only when my extremities go tingly and then numb and I'm right on the cusp of falling asleep in his arms that I realize Asher drugged me.

My own fiancé spiked my drink.

And the world goes black.

he room is fuzzy around the edges. I'm lying down. Why can't I remember how I got here? My head is still not right as I slowly wake up the next morning. Asher is long gone, probably already hard at work and not thinking about his crazy wife-to-be. The drink last night.

My upper body flings up in bed and nausea rolls. Asher drugged me. I have to take steadying breaths to not lose my stomach contents. My hand flies to my stomach.

The baby.

I hope whatever Asher drugged me with didn't hurt the baby. There're so many contraindications for pregnant women. Then again, he doesn't know I'm pregnant, so I can't blame him. I *can* blame him for taking that choice out of my hands though. He shouldn't have slipped something in my drink. Ever.

If I can't trust my best friend or my fiancé, who the hell *can* I trust?

When the nausea dissipates over an hour later, I get ready for the day, stopping in the kitchen for a piece of toast before heading out to my car. I consulted Asher's work calendar, a password he had no problem giving me a year ago. I'm not actually doing anything wrong consulting his private calendar.

I just need to speak to him.

I need to get him on my side again. I can't go into our wedding doubting if I can trust him. I can't be pregnant with his baby if he doesn't believe a word I told him last night.

Based on his calendar, he should be at the Palatio for lunch, probably wining and dining a potential donor. I'll slip the maitre d' a twenty to whisper to him to meet his wife at the bathrooms. I want him to come with me to question Ella Cooper. I want him to speak to Jack Murphy's niece. If he just looks at the evidence I've collected, I think I can get him to see why I'm feeling hunted. Like it's just a matter of time before I'm next.

I have to circle the block twice to find a parking spot. The Palatio is the place to be seen in Rosebud Grove with outdoor seating on the deck overlooking the small man-made pond. I scan the faces but don't see Asher. I check my watch and see that he should have been here twenty minutes ago. I duck inside, letting a gentleman and his date exit the crammed lobby before I can approach the maitre d' desk. A young brunette woman gives me a winning smile.

"Reservation?"

I shake my head. "No, I was hoping you could ask my husband to meet me in the bathroom area? I just need to slip him a quick note and don't want to interrupt his business lunch."

She studies me, then leans in. "I'm not sure if I'm allowed to do that, but if it's important...which one is your husband?" She shifts her head to give me a better view of the indoor seating area. The lighting is low, but enough sunshine is coming through the windows to allow me to distinguish faces. I see Asher's blond head at a table tucked in the back corner of the room.

"There…"

My voice trails off when I see who he's having lunch with. Not a donor.

Ruby.

"Ma'am?" the young girl asks, her smile slipping.

I'm suddenly so nauseous I have to twirl on my heel and dart out of the restaurant before I embarrass myself. I run into a man just entering the restaurant, but I get outside in the fresh air soon enough, gulping down one breath after another. I sag against one of the old-fashioned light poles that makes our downtown look like it's from a Hallmark movie.

Why is Asher having a romantic lunch with Ruby?

The day after he drugged his fiancée.

Are they having an affair? Is Ruby trying to kill me? Is *she* the one that's been killing off the donor recipients? To make them look like suicides so no one will question when she kills me and rides off into the sunset with my fiancé?

My heart is beating so fast my vision starts to fade around the edges. My hand lies across my stomach, as if to protect the baby that isn't even here yet from the awful truths I just uncovered. My mind is spinning.

I gasp out loud, drawing a few stares from people passing by.

"Oh God."

Could Asher and Ruby be in on it *together*? Have they been having an affair this whole time and figured offing me would be the best way for them to get together without a scandal?

I feel feverish. A little dizzy. And so, so nauseous. I lean my forehead against the light pole and beg myself to get it together. One breath at a time, I force my heart rate to slow. I count out my inhales and exhales until I feel calm. Maybe even capable.

Confidence spreads fast enough to have me opening my eyes again. The sun is shining. People are out on the street, talking, shopping, living their best lives while I fall apart alone on the sidewalk.

How dare they do this to me?

Anger spikes, cutting a path through the devastation. How dare they have an affair behind my back? Ruby is nothing but a conniving slut, stealing my fiancé when she knows he's all I've got. I almost died so many times because of my faulty heart, and now when I have a second chance, she tries to steal my future?

Fuck. That.

I will not lose Asher and this life we're building together. This baby will have a happy mother and father. Together.

Ruby's got to go.

I push my purse strap onto my shoulder and march myself back into the restaurant. The young woman opens her mouth when she sees me approaching the maitre d' desk again, but I brush right past. I'm on a mission, one she's going to want nothing to do with in a second.

Asher sees me first, his face freezing for just a split second. It's that split second that tells me I'm right about everything. He's horrified to see me here. That lopsided grin he pastes on his face as he jumps out of the booth is as fake as the red tints in Ruby's hair.

He leans in to kiss my cheek and I push his face away. He looks like a puppy who's been struck on the nose. I turn to Ruby instead.

"Hello, best friend. Or should I say *former* best friend?"

She scrambles to her feet, dressed in scrubs. She took time off work to meet with Asher. I wonder how many of his lunches she's attended over the last year or two? How many times they've snuck out together when I was recovering from my surgery. It makes me sick to even think about it.

"Nicole," she starts, her hand holding my elbow.

I swat her hand away. "Don't touch me!" I hiss, getting right up in her face. I can feel the eyes of the other patrons starting to turn in our direction, but I'm too angry to care. They forced me to act like this. They brought their affair out into the public, not me.

"You're trying to steal my fiancé? Really? You couldn't just let me have one good thing in my life, could you?" My voice is rising and it feels incredible to let it free. "Some best friend you are. How long has this been going on?"

Asher loops his arm around my waist, his voice an embarrassed whisper. "Nicole, darling. What are you talking about? Let's get out of here and discuss this like rational adults."

"No," I say firmly, still staring into Ruby's eyes with all the hatred I feel inside. "This bitch needs to know you'll never be hers. Take your purse and get the fuck out of here, Ruby. I'm the only woman who will sit with this man in a restaurant."

Ruby's face has gone pale. Good. She should feel terrible. She leans down to grab her purse, but when she straightens, she shakes her head. "I'm not who you think I am, Nicole. I'm not having an affair with Asher."

That's when I cock my arm back and punch her right in the nose for putting my fiancé's name in her mouth. Asher shouts, along with half the restaurant gasping in horror. He pulls me back, far too late. Ruby's holding her nose as blood seeps between her fingers. She runs out of the restaurant, and I watch her go with a sick glee. If there weren't so many prying eyes, I might follow her and make her really regret putting her hooks into Asher.

"Sir." A large man in a suit materializes next to us. "I'm sorry, Mr. Kingsley, but your guest needs to leave."

Asher's head is bobbing and he still hasn't let go of me, like I need some kind of leash out in proper society. He pushes me toward the front door, our pace far too quick for my liking. The poor girl at the maitre d' desk looks horrified. I flash her a smile that only makes her jaw drop further. My knuckles sting and it feels fucking glorious.

"I don't know what's gotten into you, but you're going home. Right now." Asher turns on me the second we step outside. His cheeks are as red as they are when he comes back from a ski trip. He shakes his head, looking at me like one would a cockroach unexpectedly joining you at the dinner table. Seems a little unfair considering he's the one having the affair.

"Yes, we'll definitely talk about this at home." I fumble in my purse for my keys. "I can't believe I caught you red-handed. And you drugged me last night!"

Asher shoves his hands in his hair, messing up the gelled hairstyle he spends so much time on each morning. "I can't with you." He snatches the keys out of my hands and marches to my car. "Get in, and for fuck's sake, keep your mouth shut."

I gape at him as he climbs into the driver's side and slams the door. He's never talked to me like that before. Nor not opened my door for me. Things are rapidly sliding off the rails. Our wedding is in nine days, for Christ's sake. I take a deep steadying breath and walk slowly to the passenger side door. Perhaps Asher needs to understand that I'm not leaving him for cheating on me. We'll work things out like all couples do when they have an argument.

Climbing inside, I shut the door and click my seat belt into place. Asher peels away from the curb, and I have to hold on to the handle above my head to keep from smacking my skull against the window.

"Slow down!" I shout as he speeds out of the downtown area. "This is not worth dying over. It's just a hiccup. A fixable, run-of-the-mill hiccup."

Asher slows down, mostly just to gape at me. "A hiccup?

You punching your best friend in the nose in public and accusing us of having an affair is just a *hiccup?*"

I shake my head slowly. "No. Me punching my ex-best friend in the nose is justice. You having an affair is just a hiccup." I reach over and hold his hand, the one gripping the gear knob for dear life. "I forgive you. With a little therapy and some time, we'll get through this."

Asher flings my hand off of his, scoffing. "You're unbelievable."

I turn to him with a smile, adrenaline still pumping through me. "I know."

He just gapes at me some more.

As we drive home, I think about all I've discovered today. I should be angrier at Asher, but he probably couldn't help himself. Ruby is drop-dead gorgeous, and when I was so sick from surgery, she was probably throwing herself all over him. Boys will be boys and all that. I'm disappointed, but it's not enough to make me throw away our whole future. There's a baby in this car right now who's counting on her mother and father working out their differences.

Ruby is the one I'm pissed at. A bloody nose is the least of her worries. I know who's killing the organ recipients. I just have to prove it's her and she'll be locked away for good, leaving me and Asher to have that beautiful life we've always planned.

Really, I just saved Asher from going down a horrible path.

He'll thank me one day.

Today is not that day however. When we get home, he immediately gets out a suitcase and starts throwing some clothes into it. I sink onto the bed and watch him.

"What are you doing?"

He stares at me like he's just now noticing my features for

the first time. Like he just now notices my eyes are more green than blue.

"I'm sleeping at Mother's until you've come to your senses." He zips the suitcase closed, sets it on the floor, and extends the handle.

Panic starts to set in. We can't work through this issue if he's at Josephine's. She'll poison him against me.

I jump up and put my hand on his. This time he doesn't fling me away.

"I love you, Asher. Always have and always will. I don't need time to come to my senses. Don't you see? You're it for me. I'd do anything to keep you." I reach down and grab the hemline of my dress, pulling it over my head and dropping it on his suitcase. I'm not wearing a bra and the lacy underwear I chose this morning don't have much to them.

Asher's gaze traces down my body, and I can feel the conflict rolling around in his head. I climb onto the bed and lie back. Asher swallows hard.

"Come show me I'm yours."

The suitcase is forgotten and Asher takes out his frustration with the situation on my body. I don't mind. I smile up at the ceiling, knowing I've won. Ruby is a thing of his past, which is where she'll always stay.

I'm Asher's present and future.

It just took him a little longer than me to know it.

# CHAPTER SIXTEEN

"I want her fired," I say firmly early the next morning.

Asher pauses putting on his tie in the mirror. "Nicole, nothing happened."

I shrug. I don't know if that's a lie or not, but I saw them having lunch together under false pretenses. His calendar said he was having lunch with a donor. That's enough suspicion for me to want her gone. I can't have them continuing to work under the same roof.

"I still don't trust her and intuition is everything. I'd appreciate if you'd listen to the woman you're about to marry. I have worries. I have concerns. The easiest solution is to fire her. She'll get another job somewhere else in no time. Nurses are in high demand."

Asher sighs, but doesn't disagree. "I assume she's out of the wedding?"

I nod. "Most definitely. Which is fine. I want it to be about you and me. No one else needs to stand there with us."

I come up behind him and slide my arms around his waist. My silk robe falls off my shoulder and I see his gaze trace the movement in the mirror. "Also, I need you to tell your mother she requires a different dress."

Every single one of his muscles tightens up. He turns in my arms, his hands going to my waist, though it feels like he's trying to push me away, not pull me in. "What is this about?"

I smile patiently, even though I want to scream and curse about the monster that is his mother. "She plans to wear a cream lace dress. That's very gauche and she knows it. She wants to wear it to take away from my special day and I'd appreciate if you'd steer her in another direction."

Asher drops his forehead to mine. "As much as I don't want to get involved in any of that, I like seeing you focused on the wedding."

I smile up at him, then press a kiss to his lips. I decided last night that sharing my fears about the organ recipients with Asher would be fruitless. He clearly thinks I'm panicking over nothing and sharing any of that panic with him will just result in suspicions of losing my mind and possibly more drugs dropped into my drink. I'll have to solve this mystery on my own.

"I booked a flight out to see my dad one last time before the wedding. Figured getting away from the Ruby situation would be good for my stress levels." And the health of our baby.

Asher nods, already releasing me to move on with his workday. "Good. I think that's great."

He's almost out of the room when I remind him.

"Remember. Ruby needs to be gone by the time I get back."

The look he gives me is one I haven't seen from him before. But in the end he nods.

I wait until I hear the garage door close. Then I get out my own suitcase and pack an overnight outfit and some toiletries. I'm getting on a plane, but not to New Mexico. I heard back from Colin Davis, the last organ recipient I haven't talked to yet. We agreed to meet tonight, so I have a flight to Arizona instead. I can't live with myself if I don't warn him about all of us dying, one by one. I just feel a strange pull to find him, a kinship that can't be explained. Plus, he might have the missing piece as to why this is happening in the first place.

I get to our meeting spot early, a run-down diner with cracked vinyl booths and small jukeboxes on each table that take my quarter but don't play my song selection. The bottle-blonde waitress takes my order of a decaf coffee and a grilled cheese without even looking at me. The name tag pinned to her faded pink uniform says Joy, but it's apparent that all of it has been sucked out of her over the years. I decide to leave a large tip to be the one bright spot in her day.

Colin slides into the other side of the booth before my food arrives. He's young, sporting dark hair and a spiderweb of red, raised scars down the left side of his body. His T-shirt has a hole right by the neckline.

"You Nicole?" he grunts.

I nod. "You must be Colin."

He lifts a hand for the waitress and orders the fried chicken without even looking at Joy. He doesn't say please or thank you either. My impression of Arizona is not going great so far. Hot, dusty climate and rude people.

"I asked to meet with you because I found out you and I both got an organ donation from the same man."

Colin frowns, sitting back in the booth and eyeing me like I'm going to ask him for money. Then his gaze snags on my engagement ring and he clearly changes his mind.

"What do you want?"

"Are you aware that there are six of us who got organs from the same man? And that man was a serial killer?"

If Colin is surprised or horrified, he doesn't show it. "Nah.

Don't much care who it came from. Just trying to live my life."

"And how's that going?"

Colin huffs a humorless laugh. "Terrible."

Joy clanks down a plate with my grilled cheese and limp fries. "Anything else?"

I smile up at her. "All good. Looks delicious!"

She grimaces and leaves without a word.

"You got a bone graft?" I ask, shoving a fry in my mouth. God, I love fries. Or maybe it's the baby, because I never really liked them before.

Colin watches me eat, then finally starts talking. "Yeah. Shattered my femur in a car accident. They gave me the option of titanium plates or a bone graft. I took the bone graft since they said I wouldn't need further surgeries like I would for the plates."

Joy sets down Colin's plate of fried chicken. This time she doesn't even ask if we need anything before she walks off. Colin dives in, eating an entire piece of chicken before continuing his story. I've almost finished my fries.

"I was healing pretty good too, but then I started getting these phantom pains. That's what the doc called it when I went back in. I'd get these crushing pains right where my leg had broken. Felt like I was back in the accident, waiting for the paramedics to arrive. Thought it was infected, but the doc says no. Now I wish I'd gone for the titanium."

I swallow down a bite of the grilled cheese. "Did he give you good pain meds to help you through?" Speaking of meds, I take my little pink container out of my purse and down my heart pill.

Colin talks with his mouth full. "Yeah, but it does no good. I take the pain meds, which make me sleepy, and then I dream about being beaten to death."

My stomach turns, and I have to put the rest of the grilled cheese back on my plate. "I see."

I don't see anything. I'm thoroughly confused why all of us seem to be having issues with our transplanted organs.

Except me, of course. I'm doing just fine with my heart.

"I have to warn you, Colin. Three of the organ recipients have died. Just recently. In fact, I think someone might be targeting us."

He stares at me midbite, then tosses the picked-over chicken bones back on the plate. "Targeting? As in, trying to kill us?"

I nod. "Yes. I know it sounds crazy, but I came here to warn you." I dig in my purse and pull out my phone. I unlock it and show him the screen. "Have you seen this woman?"

He only looks at it briefly. "Nah. She's hot though."

I tamp down the rage at yet another man finding my ex-best friend attractive. "She might be the one about to kill you, so maybe take her seriously."

Colin tosses his napkin on the table and sits back. "Good. Let her take me out. At least I'd have a good last view."

My jaw drops. "You *want* to die?"

He digs in his pocket, pulls a ten-dollar bill out of his wallet, and tosses it on the table. "I'm tired of fighting, lady. I'm in excruciating pain most days. And my nights are filled with nightmares. Death has to be better."

And with that, he leaves.

I DON'T SEE the news report until the next evening when I get back in Rosebud Grove. I'm curled on the sofa, a tray of lasagna keeping warm in the oven, takeout from a little

Italian place downtown. My laptop's open, searching for more information on this organ donor. I ping James again, saying I'll pay double if he can get the report to me by tomorrow. I want this mystery solved before my wedding so I can start my new life with zero worries. He doesn't answer.

That's when I see it. A small news story on the web browser page I would have looked right past just a few days ago.

*Diner waitress killed behind her place of work. Goodyear, Arizona.*

I click on the local news article and see a much younger Joy smiling in a pink work uniform and hair pulled back in an identical high ponytail. I swallow hard, immediately feeling nauseous. The article outlines how her throat was slashed when she went out the back to take out the trash. The community is scared as they don't normally see that kind of crime there.

I don't know what to feel. I didn't know Joy but I did just speak with her. Suddenly I'm very glad I tipped her a fifty-dollar bill when I got done with my grilled cheese. I hope she smiled when she saw that tip lying on the table. One bright spot in her day before her life was snuffed out.

I'm just about to close out of the computer when I see another news article further down the page. *Local man's suicide renews the city's efforts for critical mental health services.*

I click on it and end up slamming the laptop shut.

Colin Davis killed himself last night after he met with me at that diner. He swallowed a handful of pain meds and died in his sleep.

"Fuck!"

I stand up from the couch and begin to pace the living room. Colin told me himself he wanted to die. This should not be a shock, and yet it still is. What are the odds that there were six organ recipients from the same man, and now only two of us are still alive a year and a half later? I feel like I'm being stalked by an invisible force.

Is it something or some*one* that's killing us?

Only Ella and I are left.

If it's someone doing the killing, logic says I'm not killing anyone, so it has to be Ella. Right?

If it's some*thing*, then it would mean something is wrong with the organs. And if that's the case, how come I haven't felt anything?

I plop back down on the couch, mind spinning. Wait, what does Joy the waitress have to do with any of this? Why is she dead? A coincidence? Or is she part of it?

Fear overtakes logic. My hands begin shaking, and I don't think I'll be able to eat dinner when Asher gets home. I feel like there's a target on my back and no one believes me. Ruby isn't the friend I thought she was. Asher thinks I'm hysterical and need a sedative. Josephine would prefer whatever's killing these organ recipients gets to me before the wedding.

I freeze.

Josephine.

Could *she* be behind all of this? Is this some elaborate scheme to have me running for the hills and canceling the wedding? Would she go to such lengths to keep me from Asher?

I snort a laugh that's tipping into hysterics.

Yes, Josephine most definitely would.

Or it could be Ruby, trying to scare me for the same reasons. She wants Asher all to herself.

Then again it could be Ella. Why hasn't she died yet?

I don't want to think it could by my future mother-in-law or my former best friend out to kill me.

I'd rather it be Ella.

So that's who I'm going to focus on.

Then a bright idea occurs to me. I use a dark browser on

my laptop and log into Asher's hospital system. Ruby was clocked in at work yesterday. There's no way she could have killed Colin if she didn't clock out until five o'clock. She would have had to take a red-eye to Arizona and fly back before her morning shift. I scroll further and see a red bar across her employment entry. The note attached said she was fired this morning.

A small part of me feels guilty. Then the more sensible side of me roars loudly, feeling justified. The woman met in secret with my soon-to-be husband. It's better for all parties that they don't work together any longer.

I smack the laptop shut again and head for the kitchen for some lasagna. I have to keep eating for the baby's sake.

And if I track my husband's location on my phone while I eat alone at night, it feels very justified.

No one can be fully trusted.

No one.

# CHAPTER SEVENTEEN

*A*sher is purposely working late and leaving early. The only time we interact now is at night, in the dark, when we don't have to use words to connect. I'm not happy about it, but at this point, I have too much on my plate to hash out our differences. Him being gone gives me the space to investigate what the hell is going on.

We only have five days before the wedding, which means I need to go see Ella and get to the bottom of this mystery. I refuse to just sit back and be picked off like a task on a to-do list that needs to be crossed off. If Ella's behind the killings, I'll have to take her out first.

My stomach feels like it's lined with lead just thinking about taking another person's life, but in a game of her versus me, I refuse to let it be me that gets taken out. I deserve a happily ever after with Asher. I was gifted a perfectly working heart and now I have to put in the work to keep it beating. I have to do what I have to do. It's as simple as that.

I did some sleuthing last night. I'm actually quite horrified how much information you can find on the internet if you know where to look. Ella's new Washington address is only a two-hour drive away. The ride across beautiful country highways gives me time to plan out what I'm going to do. Ideally, I'd like to talk to her first. See if she's actually the one behind the deaths. Then again, if she's behind the deaths, she'll take one look at me and kill me, no conversation necessary. Perhaps I'd do better to tail her, observe without her knowing I'm there, and come to my own conclusion. Then I can kill her if need be.

That decided, I don't go to her house first. I head straight for her workplace, a little office outside of Tacoma where she's a paralegal. I have a great view across the street under the shade of a tall tree. Binoculars tell me she's an efficient worker, not super talkative, but attractive based on the number of male lawyers who find a reason to come up to her desk to chat.

A little after noon, I pull away from the curb and drive to her house, a small two-bedroom place just fifteen minutes from her job. No neighbors look to be home, though even if they were, I find that no one tends to bat an eyelash over a Mercedes in the driveway. I head for the back of the house, looking into windows to confirm no one is home. It's just dumb luck that the back door is unlocked. I shake my head, turning the knob and stepping inside. Small-town girls need to learn to always lock their doors.

Ella keeps her place tidy, I'll give her that. She has a framed picture of her and Toby, though he's barely recognizable in the picture. They look like a happy couple, her sitting on his lap in the wheelchair, big goofy grins on their faces. I don't see anything that would indicate she's the one murdering all the organ recipients, but then again, if she's a paralegal, she'd know not to keep evidence to a crime.

I pull the tiny camera from my pocket and install it on the curtain rod in her bedroom. She'd only find it if she knew to look for it. Another camera goes in the kitchen and another on her back patio. I check my phone to see that all three are working.

"Better be on your best behavior, Ella," I say out loud, my own voice echoing back to me through the app on my phone.

I close out of the app and head for my car, backing out of her driveway and heading back home. Not long after I reached my house, the app starts pinging with notifications. I click open the app and see Ella entering her home. She dumps her laptop bag in the kitchen and kicks off her heels. I spend the rest of the evening listening and watching.

Around nine, when Asher is still not home, I close out of the app and try to close my eyes. I'm exhausted, from worry about the deaths, stress regarding the impending wedding, and of course, the baby. First-trimester fatigue is a very common symptom and this little one is definitely sucking my body's resources to grow. I rub circles on my low belly, focusing on him or her instead of my worries.

My phone rings, startling me. I sit up in bed, realizing I actually dozed off. Asher's still not home. I answer the call, even though I don't recognize the phone number.

"Hello?"

"Is this Nicole Kelly?" the woman's voice asks.

"Yes, who's this?" I'm ready to hang up, nerves sparking as I consider the danger I'm in.

"This is Ann MacDonald, Emily's mother."

Recognition hits and relief floods my body. I sit back against the headboard. "Mrs. MacDonald, thank you so much for calling me back. My condolences on losing your daughter."

There's a sniffle, but Ann speaks after a moment. "I understand you were with her. In the end."

I nod. "I was. She..." I pause, unsure how to say what I need to say without offending a grieving mother. "She seemed upset. Uneasy. Could you tell me about that?"

"Oh, yes. She was definitely upset. Her transplant took so much out of her. No teen should have to go through cystic fibrosis. We thought the transplant would be the end of her medical issues when she recovered so well, but about six months ago, things took a turn for the worse."

I remember what the ER doctor told me. "Her body began to reject the lungs?"

"No. I mean, yes, eventually, but her issues started before that."

I turn up the volume on the side of my phone so I can hear her clearly. "Oh?"

"She, um, well, her mood changed. She was always a goth girl." Ann chuckles. "Always loved to wear black, our little Emily. But she was always a kind girl. Would give you the black shirt off her back. But then six months ago she got mean. She'd say crazy things in a fit of anger, then apologize for them later. It was out of character. She started going off about conspiracy theories. Her favorite was about the medical system. Said big pharma was cashing in on disease. Doctors were corrupt. Even went so far as to say she could prove a woman got put at the top of the transplant list when she shouldn't have."

I swallow a gasp. Could that be what's behind all this? Did Ella tamper with medical records and put herself at the top of the transplant list? Did on of the others somehow find out what she did and she's been killing them one by one?

"Anyway, we tried to talk her down, but she was adamant about finding this woman and making things right. We got scared. My husband always had some rifles in the house, but he got rid of them, worried she might, like, use them one day. And then, she was on your doorstep, taking her last breath." Ann's voice trails off into a sob.

I feel for her, I really do. Can't be easy to lose your young daughter like that. But I'm currently trying to save my own life, and right now, I need to get to the bottom of what Emily found.

"Does the name Ella Cooper ring a bell to you?"

Ann gasps, then blows her nose. "Yes! She had a list of names in her room that we found afterward. Ella Cooper, Jack Murphy, Toby Jackson, Colin Davis, Cyrus Bixler, and you, Ms. Kelly."

My heart is pounding far faster than it should for being seated in bed. My brain is overloaded with possibilities. So Emily knew about the organ donor. And she'd tried to come here and warn me. But warn me about who? Ella? It has to be Ella. She's the last one standing.

"Thank you, Mrs. MacDonald. I'm so sorry for your loss."

"Thank you, dear. If you find out anything, you let me know, okay?"

I agree, distracted and needing to get her off the phone so I can do more research. I'm about to fire the guy who's putting together the report on Cyrus Bixler. At this point, he's irrelevant. I need an in-depth report on Ella Cooper. Reaching over to my bedside table, I swallow the heart pill I forgot to take with dinner and check my camera app to see what Ella is up to. Sadly, it's nothing more exciting than feeding her cat and watching a late-night romantic comedy on her couch.

It's not until Asher sneaks into bed two hours later, thinking I'm asleep, that I realize something curious. Ann MacDonald had a slight Valley Girl accent, not a southern accent like her daughter.

*THE FOG CUTS off my feet, making it feel like I'm floating instead of running. Everywhere I turn, there's the fire, billowing out of control in the middle of the forest clearing. A girl screams and its shrill sound echoes in my skull. I shove my fingers in my ears but that doesn't mute the volume of her scream.*

*The fire flashes, the flames dance higher and suddenly I realize I'm the one screaming. Pain, sharp and icy, stabs at my skin. My knees buckle and I'm in the dirt, fire all around me. I drop my hands and stare at the face on the other side of the wall of fire. I know this person who watches me with glee. Know their features like I do my own. They win.*

*I'm going to die here.*

*All fight is gone. The end is now.*

*I inhale the smoke and blissfully fall unconscious.*

I awake abruptly, a scream curled in my throat. I throw off the covers and sit up, drenched in sweat. Asher stirs next to me, turning over in his sleep. My hands glide over my unharmed arms and then press against my racing heart.

"Goddamn," I whisper out loud, needing proof I'm alive and not currently burning in the middle of a bonfire.

I force myself to take long deep inhales and controlled exhales. A sound over at the window overlooking the front of the house has my head whipping in that direction. I gasp again, certain I saw a flash of Ruby's dark hair as she turned away from the ground-floor window. My body is in motion before my brain engages, moving swiftly and silently across the carpet to stare out the window.

No one is there.

I wait, each exhale fogging up the window. Five minutes go by. Then ten. And still I see no one outside. No sounds of a car firing up. No noise whatsoever in our peaceful neighborhood.

Thinking I had to have imagined it, I walk to our closet to find dry pajamas. It makes sense. That dream was intense.

Totally normal to think I saw something outside our window. Lord knows I've been paranoid the last few weeks. Maybe Asher is right. Maybe I need a nightly sedative.

There's no way I'm going to go to sleep now. Not when it feels like I downed a few dozen espresso shots. I grab my phone and pull up the camera app.

I zoom in on the bedroom camera. The bed is still made. No one in it. I switch to the kitchen app which shows part of the living room. No Ella on the couch or the floor. I zoom every which way the cameras allow me.

Ella isn't at home.

Could she have been who I saw at my window?

I jump out of bed, terrified all over again. Heading straight for the walk-in closet, I take out the fully loaded Glock my father insisted I learn how to use as a teenage girl. I used to roll my eyes, thinking his safety lessons were over the top, but now I see the usefulness.

If Ella is stalking me at my own house, she'll have to get to me before my Glock finds her. I stash it under the mattress on my side of the bed.

Needless to say, I stay wide awake until the sun begins to rise and Asher stirs next to me.

# CHAPTER EIGHTEEN

I leave the house just minutes after Asher. My loaded Glock is tucked under my seat. Not exactly legal, so I watch my speed and make sure I observe all the laws of the road out to Ella's house. Her car isn't in the driveway, so I drive right by her house and keep going, starting the route to her place of work. My knuckles start to ache with how tightly I'm gripping the steering wheel.

Murdering someone before they murder you is not how I thought I'd spend the week before my wedding, but here we are. I've tried to cover my tracks as much as possible. Private web browsers with an IP address scramble have helped me figure out the do's and don'ts of getting caught. I wore gloves in Ella's house yesterday so my fingerprints shouldn't be on anything. After I...take care of her today...I'll go immediately back to her house to remove the cameras. I even have a fake magnetic license plate to pop over my real one in case any nosy neighbors try to memorize the information of a car that doesn't belong. It's amazing what you can find on the internet.

"Oh, shit!"

I squint my eyes, thinking the lack of sleep is getting to me, but no. Ella's car is sitting in a small parking lot just a few miles from her office. It has to be her. How many people in Washington have California plates and a Hawaiian Islands sticker on the back of their black SUV? I slow my car, put on my blinker, and turn into the Eagle Glen Neighborhood Park.

"What is she doing here when she should be at work?"

I park two parking spaces down from her, darting glances around, trying to find her. There're no other cars in the parking lot. Thankfully, I'm dressed like a housewife about to go to an exercise class to keep her body toned, all in black. I slide the Glock and my newly purchased silencer into the fanny pack around my waist and exit the car. The keys dig into my palm as I walk slowly toward the playground. No kids are out yet this morning, which is a good sign. I don't need anyone remembering me.

Is Ella out for a walk? I see a trailhead to the right of the playground and head in that direction. The red dirt trail quickly leads into a forested area. My tennis shoes crunch over the brief bits of gravel used to fill potholes in the trail. Birds flit from treetop to treetop, whistling a tune. It's fairly remote out here. Looks like acres of forested land. This could be perfect. If I find her on the trail, I can surprise her, shoot her, then leave quickly before anyone else arrives at the park.

I pick up my pace, wanting to get this over with before the rest of the world wakes up and decides it's a good day to go on a walk. Except I nearly trip over a large rock embedded in the dirt. I look down and start to chastise myself about being more careful.

There's a droplet of something red in the dirt spread across the rock. I freeze, then lean down to examine it. That's got to be blood. I look left, then right. There's another drop of blood at the edge of the trail on the right. Heading in that direction, I enter the woods, following each drop of blood, the pace of the drops coming faster now. I pull out my Glock and screw in the silencer, holding it down by my side as I run.

I don't have to run far. The copse of trees gets denser around a large boulder, at least until you get to the other side where there's an open area, devoid of moss-covered trees.

I gasp and lift up the gun. My hands are shaking as I hold it. I approach the person lying on the ground, face up. Her eyes are open, unseeing and frozen in panic.

It's Ella.

There's a pool of blood at waist level, soaking into the dirt and leaves below. She's not breathing. Not moving. Her lips look blue.

I lower my gun and squat down, absolutely terrified for a different reason.

Her wrist, the one that had the scars from her skin graft, is sliced open. A knife lies nearby, covered in her blood. I shake my head and get to my feet, backing away.

My back hits a tree, my skull smacking against the trunk. It's enough to make me see stars. And to knock some sense into me.

I need to get the hell out of here.

I need to remove all evidence that I was following Ella. I shove the gun in my fanny pack and grab a small branch lying on the ground. I use it to sweep across the ground and remove any trace of my footsteps. It takes far too long as I back out, careful not to step on the blood drops. My back is aching from stooping over, but I know I have to do it.

There's a handful of various footprints on the trail, which is pretty normal for a public park. I'm not worried about my footprints being found here. I toss the branch onto the other side of the trail and speed walk back to the parking lot. I'm out of breath by the time I make it inside the safety of my car.

I force myself to leave the park at a normal speed.

Cameras are everywhere these days, and I don't need to add any suspicion by looking freaked out. I head straight for Ella's house where I slap on the fake license plate one block over, go through her unlocked back door, and remove the cameras. I'll have to review the recorded video later to see if anything unusual happened last night.

Back in the car and headed home, I finally breathe a little easier. Except I turn the corner away from Ella's house and drive right by a car that I'd know anywhere.

A silver, beat-up Camry.

The kind that sticks out in my neighborhood, but not so much here.

No one is in it.

I'm back to hyperventilating as I zoom past, no longer caring if I'm observing the speed limit or not. I have to get out of here. Now.

That was Ruby's car.

I'd bet my life on it.

And sadly, my life might just be what I'm about to lose.

They're all dead now. Except for me. Ella wasn't the killer after all.

I check my rearview mirror every three seconds, expecting to see the silver Camry following me. I'm not built for espionage though, and I'm not sure if I was being tailed, if I'd know it or not. I bounce over the curb when I turn in at my house and scream at my garage door to open faster. I zoom in the second I have clearance and immediately shut the garage door again, all the while my gaze is glued to my rearview mirror. Only when the door is down do I relax.

"Holy shit," I breathe, resting my head back.

It might take years for my heart rate to come back down into a normal range. My head is spinning.

If Ella's dead, she clearly isn't the killer.

If Ella's not the killer, who the hell is?

Why was Ruby by Ella's place? It's not anywhere near her neighborhood.

Could I have been best friends with a killer, a fiancé stealer, and I just didn't know it? Is Ruby killing these people just to toy with me? That's a level of sadistic I didn't know she had in her.

With shaky hands, I get out of the car and head inside. I check every door lock and window to make sure I'm secure. I set the alarm. The Glock stays around my waist in the fanny pack. There's no way Ruby can get in here.

Back on the couch, I pull up my laptop and open a private browser to type in one name: Ruby Evans. A long list of search hits stream down the screen and I click on every one. Most are information I already knew. Some are websites that want you to pay for a background check. I'm about to pay the money when a ding catches my attention. A notification on the bottom of my screen from my contact, James.

"Finally," I mutter, clicking on the notification.

The same process happens: my screen goes black and the curser flashes in the corner for a few seconds before his message appears.

*Sorry this took so long. Had a family emergency. Here's the report.*

Then there's a clickable link.

I don't bother responding before I click on the link. Family emergency. Sure. Someone probably paid him better and he put my request on the back burner. I know how these things work.

A full report on Cyress Gene Bixler pulls up, pages and pages of information that's not public knowledge. I settle into the couch and read through every line. I know who his parents are, what elementary school he went to, and what he prefers on his eggs. I see he went to juvenile detention for sexual assault before he even graduated high school.

"What a dirtbag."

Sadly, he's worse than a dirtbag once I get into the killings. He escalated quickly once he got out of juvie. A taste of the thrill only made him bolder. He went from sexual assault to murder in a span of six months after release. He butchered those women, some smothered and beaten, some burned alive, still others tortured for hours before he gave them the mercy of death.

I'm thoroughly nauseous, and I haven't even made it halfway through the report. It's terrifying to realize that man's heart now beats in my chest. I get up, stretch my legs, and head for the kitchen for a glass of water. I cut up an apple and munch on it, knowing I need to keep my strength up for the baby. When I'm done, I sit back down on the couch and read the second half of the report, looking for any clues that would show me why everyone who got one of his organs is dying. I'm still missing a puzzle piece, I can feel it.

Page forty-two is when I see it.

The one and only sexual assault that didn't fit the pattern. Fifteen years ago, only an hour or so away from Rosebud Grove.

Cyrus Bixler raped a young college student and she got away.

Other than the girl back in high school, she's the only one who got away with her life.

The college student?

None other than Ruby Evans.

I let out a gasp that's half cry. Ruby never told me her rapist's name. She would rarely talk about the incident. Even as my heart aches for the woman who used to be my friend, I can't help feeling like the final piece of the puzzle has come together.

Ruby's rapist is my organ donor.

She must know. She had access, just like me. She must have logged into the hospital system. Or maybe she saw the report I had printed and stashed under the couch when she stayed with me. She must have seen his name and saw all six of us who got some of his organs. She's been systematically killing us all off. Would that be justice or is it justified murder?

I slam my laptop shut and rub my tired eyes. It makes sense. I almost can't fault her for it. I'd want every last reminder of that man gone too.

Which means...I'm next.

$\mathcal{A}$sher

"OKAY, Nicole. Time to tell me your secrets."

My fiancée is gone, out getting her hair done before our big day. I scrub my hands over my face and spin in a circle, taking in our house. I left my phone in my office, just in case she tries to track me. Never thought I'd have to worry about Nicole keeping track of me. All the trust I thought we had has been blown to pieces after one lunch with her best friend.

All because we've been worried about Nicole.

I haven't been sleeping well. Some might call it cold feet before getting married. I think it's more about my fiancée acting out of character for months now. She doesn't sleep well. She bites her nails, something she never used to do. She's...sharper. Her tone. Her words. Everything about her is lined with a sharp edge. Nicole used to be so soft, a real ray of sunshine in the hospital and the Rosebud Grove community. And it's past time I figured out what's going on.

Lifting up couch cushions and opening drawers on the television cabinet, I sift through junk and find nothing that explains what's happened to her. I rummage through the kitchen and come up empty there too. Checking my watch, I see I only have thirty minutes before I need to leave for an appointment with the board. I can't be late. A few of the board members have mentioned how distracted I've been lately. I played it off on wedding-day jitters, but the truth is I'm afraid my wife-to-be is going insane.

Our bedroom produces nothing, though I find a loaded gun in one of those waist belt things women wear in the back of the closet. I knew she owned a gun. Anyone who's met her father would know Nicole's been raised around them, but I had no idea she had one loaded and not stored in a secure case. Seems more than a little reckless.

I'm rushing back out of the house when I spot the corner of a piece of white paper under the couch I already searched through. I drop to my knees and curse under my breath when I see a stash of paperwork and her laptop hidden below, shoved all the way up against the wall.

Why would Nicole hide her laptop?

I pull it all out and have a seat on the couch, already forgetting about my meeting. The pages flip quietly as I skim through a report on a Cyrus Gene Bixler. He's a very bad man apparently. I'm unsure why Nicole has this information. Then I see Ruby's name listed as one of his victims. Rage has my fingers crinkling the paper. I force my fists to relax. I can't help Nicole or Ruby if I get distracted.

I put down the paperwork and boot up Nicole's laptop. Entering her usual password only gets me a red X and a message to reenter the password.

"Changed your passwords, darling?" I say out loud.

I enter our wedding date, three days from now, and the laptop opens. She may be having a mental health crisis, but at least she's still somewhat predictable. I click through a few documents on her desktop, trying to remember the names that are listed. Looks like organ recipients. Must be the ones who have died recently. The ones she was worried about.

But it's when I click on her web browser that I get concerned. A message icon in the bottom corner has my attention. I click on it and the whole laptop goes blank.

"Shit," I mutter. Did she boobytrap her laptop? That's something the Nicole Kelly I met a few years ago wouldn't know how to do.

Then a curser in the upper left corner grabs my attention. Text suddenly appears.

*I'll get the report on Ruby Evans to you STAT. Double the fee.*

I stare at the words, completely lost. Nicole is investigating Ruby? Is this all just because I had lunch with the woman? I don't know how to prove to Nicole that nothing is going on with her best friend. We were meeting to discuss Nicole and her obsession with these other organ recipients. I would never cheat on Nicole. Ever. Yes, Ruby is a beautiful woman and she's been a good friend to me, but I'm in love with Nicole.

Prior to the last few months, I wanted nothing other than to marry Nicole and live a long life by her side. Her heart transplant was the greatest thing that could have happened. Now I'm starting to worry that her health is not as good as I thought it was. Maybe she started back to work too soon. Maybe all the wedding stress is too much.

Maybe she's right and something is happening to all these organ recipients.

I ignore the weird message and close the laptop. I check my watch and see I'm going to be late for my meeting. After I shove the laptop back under the couch, along with the Cyrus Bixler paperwork, I run to my car and speed through town, back to the hospital.

Any rational man would have walked directly to the boardroom for his meeting, but I'm a man deeply concerned about the love of his life. I head for my office instead and look up patient records. I scan Nicole's medications, not seeing anything out of the ordinary. Then I get into a different system and look up her organ donor. It's not technically a violation of patient confidentiality. As the chief of medicine, I'm allowed to be in this database. However, I'm not sure a judge would agree based on my relationship to the patient.

I enter Nicole's name and hold my breath as the results populate.

When they do, I feel like I'm sinking into my chair, sliding right down into a rock bottom I didn't know I was headed for.

Nicole's organ donor was Cyrus Gene Bixler.

She knows.

And she knows he also raped her best friend.

My head flops back on the leather chair head rest and I gaze up at the ceiling, unseeing. What the hell is going on? How does all this fit together? My brain moves the pieces this way and that, but not one clear picture emerges.

I grab my phone and shoot out a text.

Not to my fiancée, but to Ruby.

*Me: We need to talk.*

"Did you forget your meeting?" My mother's voice pulls me from my phone. "Helen is really slipping in her duties. I'll have a word with her."

My head snaps up and I shove the phone in my pocket as I stand. Mother has her bony arms crossed over her Chanel chest, tapping one heeled toe while she blocks my doorway.

"Helen is feeding the board members right now. She's doing exactly what I told her to do." I button my suit coat and push past Mother. Her heels click-clack behind me on the linoleum as we speed walk to the boardroom. Helen knows to keep them distracted when I'm late. I don't need my mother interfering with a well-oiled machine. Then again, Mother doesn't seem to know when to butt out of my business.

Right before the door to the boardroom, I turn to her. "And I need you to wear a blue dress to the wedding. My favorite color."

Her mouth pinches, making her lips look like that of a smoker's. "It's far too late to be telling me that, son."

I kiss her cheek, nearly choking on the perfume she's doused herself in every day since before I was born. "You can make anything happen, Mother."

And then I swoop into the boardroom, shaking hands and charming everyone I see. Helen has made sure they're fat and happy on homemade pastries and specialty coffee. I take a seat at the head of the table and start the presentation.

If there's one thing I'm good at, it's compartmentalizing things. As I go over the impressive financials, my mind doesn't stray to Nicole or her organ donor or my wedding in three days. I make sure the board is happy before concluding the meeting. They all stand, shaking my hand and wishing me well on my marriage. I've planned a surprise honeymoon to Hawaii afterward, so they know I'll be gone for about ten days. Mother stays, eyeing Helen as she cleans up from the meeting. When Helen finally leaves, Mother turns her sharp gaze my way.

"What's your deal with her?" I ask, sliding my computer into my bag and all the notes Helen drafted for me ahead of time.

Mother's eyebrow wings upward. I'm surprised she can still move it with all the spa appointments she makes every ninety days. Then again, even a Botoxed eyebrow would never defy Josephine Kingsley.

"You know she was your father's little toy for years, don't you?"

I grimace. "Really, Mother? I didn't need to know that."

She stands, walking toward me slowly. "All those late nights. Trips away from home. Lunches where he worked through the day. Locked office doors."

I sling the strap of my computer bag over my shoulder and walk past her. "Well, that's not happening now. She does good work for me, so I'd appreciate you stopping the death glare."

Mother's laugh lacks humor and warmth. "Rehearsal dinner is tomorrow night. Are you excited?"

I pause at the door, turning back. Mother and her sudden changes in topic. Classic behavior. I love the woman, she is my mother after all, but she can be...difficult. And that's putting it nicely. I've already had to run interference between her and Nicole so often it's become a part-time job of mine. Lately, I haven't been doing a good job of it. Distractions at work have taken my focus. Just a blip of time with my attention elsewhere and everything in my personal life is teetering on the edge of implosion.

"Of course I am. I can't wait to make Nicole mine."

Mother looks like she's sucking on a lemon. "Yes. I imagine." She walks to the door, her eyes sparkling with dark glee. "Haven't seen much of her lately. Is she doing all right?"

"She's fine. Just resting before our big day." I push open the door, needing some fresh air. Mother follows.

"Oh good. I was worried about her. She seemed a little..."

I look over at her, pretend concern painted across her face. "Seemed what?"

Mother smiles brilliantly. "A little off." And then she turns and walks the other way.

I narrow my eyes at her backside, then shake my head. Mother is just being Mother. She never cared for Nicole. Said she wasn't good enough for me. Apparently, her son marrying for love isn't ideal in her mind.

Frankly, I don't have time to deal with her today. I have a mystery to solve and a fiancée to deal with. We've gone days without talking now, longer than we've ever gone before. She isn't going to distract me with her body tonight, a tactic that I enjoy but don't appreciate when we have real problems. We're going to talk. Connect. Figure out what's going on and then fix the problem. Together.

And then in three days, we'll get married.

No more paranoia.

No more secrets.

I won't allow it any longer.

# CHAPTER TWENTY

She's not as sly as she likes to think she is.

Ruby's exiting the diner with a bag laden with takeout. Way too much food for one woman to eat alone. She's not in her typical scrubs today. Instead, she's wearing tight jeans, a dark top, and a red leather bomber jacket. With her thick hair and painted lips, she looks like she's on her way to a casual date. Asher's location is still pinging from the hospital, though he has no calendar appointments for this evening.

"It's suspicious, don't you think?" I ask out loud. No one answers, thank God. I haven't lost my mind entirely. I rub my belly and promise my little one that I'll get to the bottom of this one way or another. He or she has a bright future if I can just live long enough to marry their daddy.

I watch her get into her beat-up sedan, secure the food in the passenger seat, and then disappear behind the wheel. When she takes off from the curb, I wait a few moments, then follow her. She's driving fast like she always does. I almost lose her a few times, but I keep heading toward the hospital and am rewarded when I catch up to her. I let her park in the visitor garage before I enter behind her and find my own spot. It's not like I really need to follow her at this point.

She was fired from Rosebud Memorial.

What else is she doing back here except to visit my fiancé?

I watch from behind the wheel as she exits the garage and across the walkway to the side entrance of the hospital. She disappears inside while I try to tamp down my rage. I can't do much about her visiting Asher right now. I couldn't find my gun earlier and I know there are cameras all over this hospital. I'm sick to my stomach thinking about the two of them continuing their affair after I already caught them.

The gears grind as I messily slam the car back into drive and rush out of the parking garage. My tires squeal as I take off. I drive home entirely too fast, my heart beating more erratic than it should. I'm angry. Bitter. And so damn heartbroken.

Tears cause my vision to waver. Stoplights blur together. Only the firm desire to protect my unborn baby gets me home in one piece. The sobs come the second I step in the house. *Our* house. The house that was meant to be a sanctuary for me and Asher and our future babies. How can he be doing this to me? To our future? How can my best friend?

When I need them most, when my very life hangs in the balance, they've turned on me.

I cry until my throat aches and my eyes burn. Waiting up for Asher, each tick of the clock breaks my heart. Instead of confronting the danger like I've been doing, I feel small. Powerless. Defeated. I'm just so *tired*. So tired of fighting for what's mine all the time.

So I curl up in bed and close my eyes. If I can't see the danger and betrayal all around me, maybe it'll go away. It's a naive thought, one I used to have as a little child as I hid in the dark, but now I revert to that type of thinking just to survive another night.

Tomorrow.

Tomorrow I'll face it all.

EXCEPT WHEN I wake the next morning, there's no one to confront.

Asher didn't come home.

A new onslaught of tears come with a wave of rage so strong my knees almost buckle when I stand up from the bed.

Ruby's.

That's where he must be.

That must be the person who convinced him not to come home to me.

I tear the closet apart and still don't find my gun. I don't know where I put it, which is not like me. Instead, I strap a knife to my belt loop and drop one in my purse. Thinking of the baby, I stop in the kitchen to eat the last apple in the refrigerator and drink a cup of decaf coffee. I've forgotten to go grocery shopping or do any of the mundane tasks of living. I don't, however, forget to take my heart pills. The bottle is getting dangerously low. I need to remember to stop by the pharmacy before the wedding.

The mirror by the front door catches my attention. My reflection shows a pale woman who looks like she needs a couple nights of sleep before she can be considered human, but her eyes hold fire. My hair is gorgeously highlighted thanks to the hairdresser yesterday, looking naturally sun-kissed even though I haven't been out in the sun for years.

The ring on my finger reflects the morning sunlight coming through the front window, reminding me that everything I've always wanted is within grasp.

In two days, I marry Asher.

In two days, I *will* marry Asher.

Mark my words.

I race out the door, adrenaline and righteous anger fueling me. The ride to Ruby's duplex is a blur. With each block I pass, confidence floods all rational thought. I have to take out Ruby before she steals everything from me. That's the only way to end things. She deserves it. I deserve it.

Asher's car isn't on the street when I pull up to her place. He probably left early to head to the hospital like always. Doesn't mean he didn't stay over here last night though. I'm grateful, as his absence will make what I have to do easier.

I pat the knife at my waist, making sure it's easily accessible. I flip down the visor in my car and give myself a pep talk.

"You have to do this. Life has been hard for you, and not only do you now have a new heart and a future, you have a fiancé. Everyone looks up to Asher. You have respect. You have financial security. And once Ruby's out of the way, you'll have Asher's full attention. He's a man. A stupid man with straying eyes, but under all that he's a good man. One who will make a good father." I rub my still flat belly and take a deep breath. "You have to kill her. Don't think about it. Just do it. It's the only way."

The visor makes a smart snap as I slap it back into place and step out of my car. I round the hood and walk up to Ruby's half of the duplex. I take a second to school a contrite smile on my face, one that will get Ruby to open the door and let me inside. Lifting my arm, I knock, the sound loud in the morning stillness.

Her footsteps echo on her tile floor before she opens the door. Her eyes widen for a second, but she doesn't slam the door in my face. Her hair is tousled like she just got out of bed, her pajamas silky and revealing all her luscious curves. She puts one bare foot on top of the other and leans into the door.

"Nicole. I didn't expect to see you here."

*I bet you fucking didn't.* "I thought we should talk."

Ruby stares at me for a beat before dropping my gaze and nodding. She steps back and I enter her place, inhaling deeply through my nose. I swear I can smell Asher's aftershave. Anger pulses hotter than the nerves.

Ruby follows me as I walk into her living room, the place I figured would be best to carry out what I have in mind. The neighbor she shares a wall with is frequently out of town for work, so I don't have to worry about making noise. I do have to strike quickly though. The element of surprise is paramount, given that she's stronger than me.

"Do you mind if I close these? I have a splitting headache." I point to the drapes covering her front windows. She nods, looking at me with concern instead of suspicion. Perfect.

Once I close the curtains, I have a seat on the chair and she sits on the couch. She puts her hands between her knees and leans forward.

"I'm not having an affair with Asher. I'll strap on a lie detector test if you'd like."

I nod, not accepting her denial in any shape or form. "And yet you had secretive meals with him."

She has the grace to look contrite when she nods. "I did. We were worried about you and wanted to chat, be a united front. See what we could do to help."

I notice she didn't deny having multiple secret meals with Asher. I knew it. I knew they had dinner together at the hospital last night. A calm blanket of rage floods my veins.

Killing her is justified. Cheating with your best friend's fiancé is despicable. A jury would agree.

Not that I intend to get caught.

"I've told you repeatedly that I'm fine. I shared the details about the organ recipients in confidence, and at the first available opportunity, you broke that confidence. Do you see the issue I have here?" I manage to say calmly.

Ruby's thumbs start picking at the polish, a sure sign of anxiety. "In some cases, when I believe a life is in danger, I think it's morally okay to break a confidence. And that's how I feel about you, Nicole. I'm worried for your life. Your mental stability."

I nod, not buying it for a second. She wants what I have. A big house, a fancy car, a handsome fiancé. She told me so one day when we went out to the bar. How jealous she was of my life and yet how happy she was for me. She literally told me. I just didn't listen. I had no idea she'd try to steal it all for herself.

I go to stand, to get in a better position for what I planned in my head over and over this morning, but Ruby keeps talking.

"I followed you, you know."

My gaze snaps to hers, confused.

She tilts her head. "I followed you the other night and you went straight to that woman's house. The woman who died in the forest? Ella?" Ruby's eyes fill with tears. "Was it you? Did you actually kill her?"

I'm stunned silent. My mouth opens but nothing comes out. She's trying to blame this on *me*? I jump to my feet.

"No! I didn't kill Ella! Have you not been listening to me? All the organ recipients are dying. I've been telling you this and you've been acting like I'm fucking psycho for being afraid."

She opens her mouth to argue. As quickly as I can, I slide the knife out of my waistband and knock Ruby to the floor with a backhanded jab. The butt of the knife handle adds some heft to the blow. She yelps, her body sliding off the couch and onto the floor. She holds her hand over the side of her head, and when I blink, I see dark red blood start to seep through her fingers. It feels like I'm in a dream. My lungs are heaving, in and out, in and out. Stars start to form at the edge of my own vision. I blink again, trying to keep my shit together.

Ruby turns her face upward, looking at me with astonishment. Her hand, the one she holds up in the air in some sort of lame defense, is shaking. "Nicole!"

I stand over her, sure to stay far enough away she can't kick me. I point the knife at her, feeling powerful, even if my knees are trembling slightly. "You killed all those people! You, Ruby! The man who gave us the organs was your rapist! I know, okay. Cut the shit!"

Ruby's mouth gapes open. We both pause, staring at each other as we breathe heavily. If I wasn't so sure of everything, I'd think she was genuinely surprised about who my organ donor is.

"Nicole," she breathes. Then her eyes close for a protracted moment. When she opens them again, tears seep out of the corners, streaming into her hairline.

I don't want to see her tears. I don't want to hear her excuses. She's been killing people. And trying to steal my fiancé. There's nothing she can say to make things right.

So I pounce. I straddle her and sit on her stomach, the breath whooshing out of her. Her eyes seem to bulge out of her head as she realizes what's happening. I hold the blade to her throat and lean over her.

"I don't know how you hid your true self for so long," I whisper in her face.

Ruby hisses as I dig the blade into her neck a little harder.

Tears are streaming down her face now, snot dripping from her nose. She starts to struggle, but it's weak and pathetic, just like her. "I didn't. I didn't...Nicole. I haven't hurt anyone."

Even now, when she has just seconds to live, she denies it all. Unbelievable. I shake my head and lean in one last time. Power surges through me, a warm blast of something not altogether human. It's my divine right on this earth to take this woman out of it. To slowly drain the life until she's nothing but a sack of skin and bones and useless organs. I feel better than all the pain meds the hospital has to offer.

"Rot in hell, bestie."

I push on the blade just a bit more, uncertain of the pressure needed to slice through one's throat. Blood trickles from her neck, warm and sticky. Give me a needle and I know exactly what pressure is needed, but not even nurses understand the cutting power of a hunting knife.

Ruby's eyes go impossibly wide. She stops struggling, as if she's accepted her fate. "I love you," she whispers.

I pause, horrified and disgusted. *That's* what she chooses as her last words? All that rage that powered me to follow through with her killing seeps from my pores, leaving me feeling scared and shaky.

Damn her.

We stare into each other's eyes and time stands still.

# CHAPTER TWENTY-ONE

$\mathcal{A}$sher

THE PAIN in my shoulder is sharp, honing my attention to the matter at hand. The front door bangs open on the second try, splintering wood everywhere.

"Ruby!" I yell, running into her duplex like it must be on fire. When I pulled up to her place, having tracked Nicole's location here, I saw the drawn curtains and knew deep in my gut that something terrible was about to happen. I hoped to God I wasn't too late.

A whimper hits my ears just a split second before I turn the corner and see both women on the floor, Nicole straddling Ruby with a knife against her throat. I don't think. I don't stop to analyze the situation.

I throw my whole body against Nicole in a dive that will surely hurt us all. Nicole's breath whooshes out of her body in a deep grunt. Somewhere in the back of my mind I know tackling her is not going to be good for her heart, but desperate times call for desperate measures. Our bodies roll as I try to take the brunt of the impact, but ending with Nicole pinned under me. Her knife goes clattering away on the tile floor. Ruby yelps behind us and scrambles to her feet.

"I'm calling 911!" she shouts.

"No!" I bark, looking down at Nicole. She's gone pale, her eyes so wide I'm not sure if she's going into some kind of cardiac arrest. Taking my weight off her torso, I keep her arms pinned above her head. I'm sitting on her thighs so she can't kick me.

Ruby runs to the kitchen and comes back with a gun trained on Nicole. Her neck is covered in blood and so is the side of her head. She holds a dish towel to her temple, the gun trembling so badly I'm confident she'd miss and hit me if she tried to shoot it.

"Stop. There's no need for any of that." My tone brooks no argument.

I had enough time to think about things on the ride over here from my parents' house, where I stayed last night. I knew Nicole was having issues, but what I saw this morning has shaken me to my core. Along with the gun I took from her closet, I took a set of three cameras. I had no idea what they were or where they'd been installed, but they had some drywall still attached to them, so I knew they must have been used. I downloaded an app and pulled the footage.

I just about lost my breakfast when I saw the images on my phone. Seeing Nicole train her gun on a woman and drag her out of her house by her hair changed my world view. What was up is now down. What was my future is now something I want in my rearview mirror. The person I thought was good is actually a monster.

I look down at Nicole, the woman I'm supposed to marry in two days, and only see a shell of a human.

"What the hell have you done?" I whisper.

She finally blinks and then her whole body begins to shake with tremors. I squeeze her wrists when she tries to block me out by closing her eyes.

"Look at me!" I yell.

Her eyes fly open and she tries to thrash beneath me. I press down harder and she stills. Ruby shifts, having a seat on the couch, a gun still pointed in our direction. The doctor in me wants to attend to her injuries, but I have to keep Nicole subdued first. Figure out what the hell to do with her.

"What did you do?" I ask louder this time.

Tears are leaking out of her eyes, but she lifts her chin defiantly. Her voice is choppy when she speaks. "I broke into the hospital records. I found out my donor is a serial killer. The same man who raped Ruby."

My head whips up. Ruby stares back at me, then nods quickly in agreement. I look back at Nicole, needing more explanation than that.

"I've been trying to warn them," she pleads. "I've gone to see them all, but they kept dying. Suicides, suspicious deaths." She sobs and then collects herself. "I've been so scared. And then…I saw Ruby. After I tried to track down Ella. Ruby killed her!"

I'm thoroughly confused now.

"Ella?"

"The woman who got a skin graft. She was murdered in the woods. Made to look like a suicide. Ruby was *there*. Ruby killed her like she killed all the rest of them! She's killing off all of us who got that man's organs!" Nicole explodes, nearly spitting on me to get the words out fast enough. She struggles again, trying to get her hands free.

I look over at Ruby to see she's put the gun down on the couch beside her to dab at her temple. She meets my gaze and doesn't back down either. She explains, her voice monotone, stunned and out of body. "I followed Nicole that night.

That's why I was there. I followed her to Ella's house where they stayed for a bit, and then when they left in the middle of the night, I followed her to that park. I should have gotten out of my car, but I was afraid. Nicole came running out less than an hour later and got in her car, zooming away. I waited until daylight to try to track the woman. Oh, I found her, all right." Ruby shakes her head, looking pale. "She was dead. I'm the one who called 911."

"That's not true!" Nicole cries.

"Are you kidding me?" Ruby shouts over her.

"Enough!" I shout above them both as they begin to argue.

They both fall silent and I have just a sliver of time to think. To process. To figure out how to get out of this mess unscathed. I have enough of my mother in me to know this is going to be the scandal of the decade. The chief of medicine's fiancée has been going around killing people? I'll have to leave this town. Change my name. Start over. The shame and gossip will kill my parents.

I lift my head and pin Ruby with a glare. "Go get rope. Or duct tape. Now!"

She gets to her feet and sways. Then walks off to get what I asked. I look down at Nicole, still shattered that the woman I love is involved in this whole thing.

"I reviewed your meds."

She blinks up at me, her lower lip trembling. I shake off the urge to comfort her.

"One of them has the side effect of blackouts."

She digests that, falling still beneath me. Ruby walks back in with a roll of gray duct tape in her bloodstained hands.

"Wrap up her ankles and then I'll get her hands. Then you need to let me take a look at your injuries."

Ruby hesitates for a moment, then does what I asked. "What are we going to do with her?"

I wait until Nicole's ankles are wrapped in tape and then I get off of her. She groans and I know my weight had to have been painful. I take hold of her wrists again, seeing the red marks I've already made on them. I run my thumb across one mark, a useless feeling of remorse flitting through me, and then get busy wrapping them in duct tape. Once she's seated with her bound hands behind her and her back against the chair where her purse is lying, I help Ruby to her feet and follow her into the kitchen to grab her first aid kit. I can keep an eye on Nicole from here.

"What are we doing?" Ruby whispers.

I dap a cotton ball soaked with hydrogen peroxide against the cut on her throat. She hisses but lets me continue. The cut isn't deep, but the placement of it would have been almost instantly lethal if she pressed down hard enough. The thought of that makes me weak.

"We have to take her back to our house. Give us time to think this through. To plan."

Ruby grabs my wrist. "We have to call the police, Asher. She murdered that woman. Maybe all of them."

The gravity of the situation makes me nauseous. "I know. But think this through. If we go public with what she's done, it'll be the scandal of the century. You and I both will have to leave Rosebud Grove. Start over somewhere else. All because of what she's done. I don't want that for you or for me. Nicole's name will be dragged through the mud. She'll face a long trial. Years in jail, if not her whole life." My throat tightens and I have to inhale and exhale a few times to clear the emotion. "Even if she's done these horrible things, I don't want that for her. If she's done these things because of a medication, it's not really even her fault. She's led a hard life already. Does she deserve to rot in prison?"

Ruby releases my wrist, her own eyes flooding with tears.

"Maybe. Maybe not. I'd rather a jury decide that than you and me."

I shake my head, certain of our path forward. "No. We have to do the hard thing, Ruby. We can't let someone else determine her fate and ours along with it."

We stare at each other for a long minute before Ruby closes her eyes and gives me a slight nod. That's confirmation enough for me. I go back to dabbing the hydrogen peroxide on the gash on her temple until it's cleaned up and finally bandaged.

"Help me get her back to my house and then we'll come up with a plan. Okay?" I hold my hand out to Ruby.

She takes it without hesitation and we walk into the living room hand in hand to face Nicole. Her gaze slides down to where we're connected, tears streaming down her cheeks.

"I knew it."

I release Ruby's hand and shake my head. Then I reach down and haul her limp body over my shoulder.

"You know nothing, Nicole. It's always been you."

She doesn't speak again until I have her situated in the back seat of Ruby's car in the attached garage, about to close the door. "I loved you and you betrayed me," she whispers, tears sliding down her cheeks.

I lean in close, taking in every detail of the face I memorized over the years of loving her. "No, darling, *you* betrayed *me.*"

And then I close the door on her and the life I thought we'd have together.

# CHAPTER TWENTY-TWO

omorrow's my wedding day.

I have a new, healthy heart, but it aches so badly I fear it's going to give out on me. The stress of everything can't be good for me. I've been awake almost all night, crying on and off until my eyes hurt and I ran out of tears. They put me in the guest room last night and left. The room I intended to paint once I knew the sex of the baby. The room that would have been a nursery to hold our baby. The start of our family.

How can they do this to me? I can only imagine Ruby and Asher are together in my bedroom. How can they shack up in my house while I'm still in it? Feet and hands tied together like an animal. They're monsters! My emotions vacillate between profound sadness at the life I'm losing and rage so consuming time suspends and all I can imagine is how I'd kill them both if given just a sliver of a chance.

I've tried to slip my wrists out of the thin ropes they used to tie me to the bedposts, but they did too good of a job. The skin is raw and angry from trying to escape. My feet are still tied together with duct tape and are pretty useless without hands to rip the tape off. They confiscated my purse and phone and any weapons.

Somewhere in the early hours of dawn, I realized that my dad is flying in today for the rehearsal dinner. When he doesn't hear from me, he'll be suspicious. Will he call Asher? Will he come over and demand to see me? He's my only hope at this point.

The sun begins to stream through the crack in the curtains and I know it must be morning. My heart starts to hammer in my chest, as if I'm running a marathon when I'm simply lying in bed. With alarm, I realize I didn't take my heart medication last night. I snort. Not that I could when I'm tied up. I try to slow my breathing and will my heart to find its rhythm again. My body feels like it's floating, in a haze between sleep and awake. Visions of blood and knives and guns and fire flip through my brain like a horror show. They do nothing to calm my heart but I'm oddly drawn to them. I hold them in my head like a lovely memory that sustains me through the hard times.

Being tied up in my own house is definitely hard times. I could use some small measure of comfort, as bizarre as it is.

The door flings open with a bang, and I shriek in fear. I scramble into a more upright position, blood flow flooding my arms and making them tingle and ache. Asher enters the room, his blond hair a disaster. Bags have formed under his bright blue eyes. He looks at me as if he's shocked to see me there.

"You put me here," I remind him, my voice nothing but a croak.

He blinks, then looks down at the tray in his hands. The bottle of water catches my attention. I'm so thirsty. So hungry. He puts the tray on the dresser across the room, and

I can't help but still admire him. He's always been so hand-some. Athletic, tall, strong. A firm jawline and thick hair. A heart of gold and a true leader. I used to be the envy of the hospital, catching the eye of Asher Kingsley.

Look at me now. Tied up and helpless as I watch him leave me for my best friend.

"Am I your prisoner now?" I ask, honestly needing to know what's going on here. Reality can't be worse than my speculation. My lips crack with the movement. "I wasn't going to kill her."

It's a lie. And I think he knows it when his full lips turn down at the corners. "Shut up," he snaps.

I blink. He never used to talk to me like that. It's an unwelcome change. It also doesn't bode well for my future.

He approaches suddenly and I flinch backward. He shakes his head like he's disappointed and extends the water bottle, a straw poking out of the top. He holds it steady, and after a moment of hesitation, I dip my head and drink hungrily. I wanted to defy his measly act of kindness but basic dehydra-tion has won out.

He pulls it away from me before I'm satisfied. "Careful. Too much and you'll make yourself sick." He crosses the room to put the bottle back on the tray and leans his body against the dresser, arms folded across his chest. His familiar eyes bore into mine, as if he can see into my skull and find the answers he seeks. "What the hell is going on, Nicole? Explain it to me so I understand."

I close my eyes for a moment, exhausted beyond anything I've experienced before. Except visions of pain and blood and screaming greet me when my lids are closed. I fling open my eyes and wonder if I'm truly losing it.

"I told you already. Ruby found out her rapist donated organs. I happened to be one of them. She's been systematically killing them one by one in a sick act of revenge. I simply decided I wasn't going to let her kill me. I had to kill her first." I lift my gaze from the bedspread to see a stone-faced Asher. "I have too much to live for."

I see the way my words affect him. His arm muscles tighten and his expression shifts to one where he's in pain. When he speaks, it's a whisper that tears at my soul. "I want to believe you, Nicole. I really do."

Hope fills my chest. I sit up as straight as I can against the pillows and will him to look at me. To see that it's not too late to untie me and jump right back into our plan to get married. To be the family we always dreamed of being. We don't have to let Ruby's actions take all that away from us.

Asher lifts his head. "But I found receipts."

I screw up my face. What the hell is he talking about?

He pushes off the dresser and takes one step toward me before stopping. "I found plane tickets, receipts from gas stations, even a toll charge. All of them line up to place you in each town one of the organ recipients lived in. All right before their death."

"I know! I told you! I was trying to warn them someone was killing us off!" My hair is sticking to my neck. God, it's hot in here. My heart is beating so fast now I can barely hear myself over the thud-thud-thud.

Asher shakes his head. "I tracked Ruby's movements too. Except for Ella, she was at work over the dates those people died. There's no way she could have killed them."

I do not accept his words. He's wrong. He has to be wrong. I pull on my restraints and scream in frustration. "No! She did it! Not me. *Her*. Let...me...go!"

A sharp sting in my arm punctures my hysteria and I freeze mid-rant. Asher is right next to me, an empty syringe in his hand. I stare up at him in disbelief.

"Did you...?" The room starts to waver behind him. "Drug me? Again?"

Asher's lips press together. "It's for your own good."

I start to shake my head but it makes me dizzy. "Not... good...for the..." My words trail off as my lips refuse to move. I want to tell him to stop that. Those drugs aren't good for the baby. He needs to know. Maybe if he knew about the baby, he'd see that the life we want is already happening.

He looms over me, his handsome face now terrifying as my limbs start to lose feeling. "You should know I've canceled the wedding. Your dad's not coming. I'll take care of all the details with the various vendors. You just sleep. When you're calm again, we'll talk."

Oh God, Dad's not getting on that airplane. Asher's mother must be ecstatic at this change in plans. I'm angry, so impossibly angry, but in the back of my brain, I register that my heart has finally slowed down. My body melts into the bed below me and Asher's face gets fuzzy. I beg him to reconsider with my eyes, but he doesn't relent. His jaw only grows impossibly harder. He's not the loving, doting fiancé any longer. Any hold I had over him is long gone, stolen by my best friend.

He's no longer in my field of vision, his handsome face replaced by the ugly ceiling fan I always had plans to change. I scream at my eyeballs to move but they don't respond. I hear a female voice and struggle to stay awake long enough to hear what she has to say. But it's like my body isn't attached to my brain any longer. Dark spots steal parts of my vision.

"Did she admit to it?"

"Not yet. I had to drug her to get her to calm down."

"We need to come up with a plan." It's Ruby. It has to be her. "We have to get rid of her."

A sea of black overtakes me.

And the dreams begin.

Blood.
Pain.
Screaming.
Eyes pleading with me to help while I watch the life drain from their body.

# CHAPTER TWENTY-THREE

I no longer know what time it is. Or what day. I've slept, I've woken up and then slept again. Asher has been in the room at several points, that straw back between my lips offering sweet relief. At some point, I dreamed of eating bread. Now I don't know if that's real or fake, but I'm leaning toward real as my hunger has dissipated. My left arm is killing me. I have a bad feeling he's continued to drug me.

There's no light coming through the edges of the drapes. I blink slowly, trying to come out of the fog. Looking down my body, I see that someone has changed my clothes on my lower half. A pad lies under me too, one of those puppy pads for dogs that aren't trained to go outside yet. I register that I should be embarrassed, but I feel nothing. I've clearly peed my pants at some point, but that's what Asher gets for keeping me tied up. For keeping me inhumanely on what should be our wedding day.

I blink again, a single tear sliding down my temple and into my hairline. Has our wedding day already passed? How much time have I spent in a semiconscious state? What does he plan to do with me?

My heart begins to pick up its pace, its rhythm no longer in sync with life. It's an irregular beat I know can't be good. I try to think back and come up with nothing but darkness and dreams. Did Asher give me my heart pills? I can't trace back the last time I remember taking them.

I pull on my hands and hiss at the sting on my wrists and the ache in my shoulder joints. I squeeze my eyes shut and tell myself to calm down. To breathe normally. I can't figure out a way out of this mess if I'm in a panic. Except my brain doesn't cooperate.

Flashes of Emily MacDonald come to me unbidden. Her dark-rimmed eyes pleading with me to listen to her. The rasp of her inhales, the shudder of her lungs. I see her on the ground, my welcome mat beneath her. I see myself calling emergency dispatch and telling them to come. I hang up and set the phone aside to hover my hands over her chest, ready to perform CPR. Except I don't push on her chest to keep her heart going. I just push down slowly, firmly, unrelentingly.

Her ribs struggle against the weight of my hands, her eyes going wide as she stares up at me in horror. Her hands grab my wrists, but she has no strength. I push until I fear her ribs might fracture. I push until the death rattle of her last breath leaves her body.

And then the sirens light up the night sky.

I sit back on my heels and smile down in triumph. Her chest no longer lifts and falls. Her eyes stare up vacantly. She's gone. Her lungs no longer the gift of life, but the bringer of death. It's poetic, really. The paramedics arrive just as I pretend to do CPR. I play my part, crying, confused, and remorseful for not being able to save the stranger who wound up on my doorstep.

"So, you did kill Emily."

My eyes fling open and Ruby stands across the guest room, her hands twisting together in front of her. Asher is next to her, standing far too closely for my liking. Ruby's words penetrate my exhausted brain. Have I been talking out loud? Why am I having these visions? They seem so incredibly real.

"No," I whisper, voice so rough I don't recognize it anymore. "No, I would never."

But they don't believe me. They press their lips in a straight line and shake their heads like I'm a monster. They leave me alone again, confused and sweaty and starting to feel like I might be having a true medical event. My heart is still not beating in rhythm. I need my pills. I kick my heels into the bed and scream for them, but no one comes back. I lie back down, chest heaving and mind scrambling. I would give anything for some more water right now.

Time passes and reality flickers in and out. Gaps of time bend my mind. I'm not sure what's real anymore. Darker images accost the back of my eyelids.

Memories? Or nightmares?

A red tiled roof, an older man with scars on one side of his face. His torment palpable as he cried. Me, comforting him while insisting ending his life was the only way to solve his problem. I didn't even do anything, not really. Just stood there to witness the man's last breath after he wrote a note explaining it all. To see the pain and anguish leave the second he dug that knife into his neck. To push his hand a little harder to end it quickly. Humanely.

I helped. Always a helper.

Just like I helped Toby. He didn't want to live without Ella. He didn't want to live his life in a wheelchair. He was losing his mind. Clearly. The man reached for me, jerked me off my feet. Incredible strength. I had to push him off me. The man would have raped me. I had to knock him out of his chair and bash his skull into the fireplace hearth. It was either him or me, and I'd never let it be me.

I wake up drenched in sweat, heart hammering. My vision swims before me. Asher and Ruby stand on either side of my bed, looking down at me like I'm a science experiment.

"How could you, Nicole?" Asher whispers.

His face swims back and forth. I wish he'd stand still. It's making me nauseous. "Had to." My voice is barely audible. "Had to save myself."

My eyelids are slowly lowering. I can't muster the strength to hold them up. Asher leans over me, his fist in the mattress. "I haven't been giving you the tacrolimus."

That gets my attention. I need my heart pills. Why isn't he giving them to me?

"You're starting to remember all those times when you blacked out," Ruby pipes in.

She's wrong. I never blacked out. I'm just having nightmares.

"No!" I scream as loudly as I can, over and over. Even so, it's mostly just a hoarse shriek.

The sting in my shoulder comes again. Darkness sucks me in and the nightmares continue, this time of a young man in his car, startled when I slip into his passenger seat. I offer him the pills, the ones I haven't been taking for the pain. I'm stronger than all that. Clearly Colin Davis isn't. He only hesitates a moment before he scoops the pills out of my palm and tosses them back. I wait with him while they take effect. He makes very little noise. Only a few jerks of his limbs in the end. I don't call 911 or attempt any life-saving measures. He wanted it this way. Death is a sweet mercy.

Except when I get out of the car, that damn waitress is there, her mouth open in shock, eyes all knowing. She's seen too much. When she runs, I have to follow.

The alley in the back of the diner is disgusting. Dirt,

grime, and a few rats finding their supper. But it's dark. A perfect place to make sure my perfect life doesn't unravel because of an unsmiling bitch named Joy. Her blood spilled all over my favorite coat. It was unfortunate, for sure.

But I had to kill her.

"You never have to kill anyone, Nicole."

Ruby's face is ashen as she leans over me. She shakes her head, tears spilling from her eyes. I remember the first time I saw her on the surgical floor, getting her ass chewed out by some egotistical doctor who never learned to grow up. I intervened with a joke that diffused the situation. Ruby had looked at me with a sheen of tears in her eyes then, beyond grateful. We'd been friends ever since.

"What happened to you, Nic?"

A sudden rush of emotion hits me, making my own eyes burn hot. I'd rather Asher plunge that syringe in my shoulder again than feel this.

"I'm sorry," I whisper, meaning it with every fiber of my being.

Ruby sobs and Asher pulls her away. She buries her face in his chest as he hugs her. I see his hand stroke the back of her dark hair. I know how calming his hand can be. He should be touching me. Not her. Never her.

Rage blows through every ounce of regret I felt a moment ago.

"No!" I scream, back bowing off the bed. "Get off of him, you bitch!"

Ruby jolts in Asher's arms, looking over her shoulder at me with alarm. He ushers her out of the room, not even giving me the gift of oblivion in the form of drugs.

I lie there for what feels like hours, dehydrated and increasingly delusional. Nightmarish memories accost me while my heart thumps just a little bit harder. My mind plays tricks on me, but one thing is now becoming clear.

I think I killed those people. Every single one of them. In one way or another.

It's a realization that takes me by surprise. I'm both horrified and proud, the two emotions swirling around, fighting for dominance. At some point, I stare up at the ceiling fan and smile. I finally figured out the puzzle. I knew I would eventually.

So, does that make *me* the monster?

Or am I just a lab rat caught up in the same serial killer DNA that ended their life too?

sher

"NONE OF THIS IS YOUR FAULT." Ruby's hand slides across my back, her soft voice trying to pull me back from the brink. My head drops, eyes squeezed shut against the dull headache that's plagued me for days now. If only I could block out all that's happened.

"It's partially my fault. How could I not see what was happening to my own fiancée?"

Shame slams into me. How many times did I disparage my father for ignoring my mother over the years? I always vowed I'd never have a marriage like that and yet here I am, stunned by the behavior of a woman I was supposed to marry today. I didn't listen, just as guilty as my father.

Ruby pats my back and then has a seat on the barstool next to me. Her eye is swollen and starting to turn a hideous shade of black and blue. Nicole did that. I did that by not stopping her sooner. If I hadn't arrived at Ruby's house when

I did, would Nicole have killed Ruby? I honestly think the answer is yes.

"I didn't want to believe it either. I even followed her to that park. Saw her and Ella go into the woods and I didn't try to stop her. I was…too stunned, I guess." Ruby trails off, lost in her own thoughts about this horrific situation.

My phone vibrates again but I ignore it, just like I have all the other messages and voicemails. Calling off one's wedding the night before is enough of a scandal as it is. If everyone in Rosebud Grove knew the extent of it, they'd be stunned.

"It's your mother. Need to get it?" Ruby says.

I lift my head, the headache beginning to pound. Even my eyes feel like they're full of sand. I see Mother's name on the phone screen and swipe it away to voicemail. I can't listen to her gloat about being right about Nicole. She never wanted us to get married, that much was obvious.

Ruby sighs, then stands up to head for the freezer where she takes out another frozen bag of vegetables and holds it to her temple. Here I am complaining of a headache and Ruby is the one with a concussion. I stand up and pour us both a glass of water. She and I both take sips, neither of us feeling particularly hungry. She taps her nail against the glass and then looks at me.

"What are we going to do?"

It's the question that's been swirling in my head since the second I broke down Ruby's door and found my fiancée about to murder our friend. It's been almost forty-eight hours and I'm no closer to finding an answer. How does one cover up one's fiancée turning into a serial killer all of a sudden?

I set my glass down and answer her as honestly as I can. "She tried to kill you. I think we have to come to an agreement on what to do with her together. Do you want to press charges?"

Ruby studies my face with her one good eye. "I don't want

her to pay for all of it, but I do want her stopped." Her good eye swims with tears suddenly. "I think she had one moment of clarity when she had me pinned down. I could have sworn I glimpsed her old self when I told her I loved her. She froze, like she couldn't go through with it."

Immediately, I shake off that sentiment. As sweet as it sounds, I fear it's incredibly naive. Nicole killed multiple people already. She would have killed Ruby too if I hadn't intervened. Of that I'm certain.

I rub my hands together, thinking out loud. "If we turn her in to the police, it will be a major scandal. My name will be dragged through the mud, as well as my family's. We'll have to testify against her. The board will probably ask for my resignation. You've already been fired. We'll probably both have to move away from here to get any kind of peace."

Ruby sniffles, still tapping her fingernail against the glass. "I can't believe this is happening."

I don't know if it's the surgeon background, where life-or-death situations must be dealt with swiftly, or just my nature, but I don't feel there's any purpose to wallowing in the surprise and shock. Action is what is needed here.

"Or..." I know this is crazy, but every which way I turn it around in my head, it's the only outcome that makes sense in the long run. "Now, hear me out."

Ruby puts the frozen vegetables down and gives me her full attention. Even with a black eye and a thin scab slicing across her neck, she's beautiful.

"What if we make it look like a suicide? It would fit the pattern of the other organ recipients. It would bury all the other murders. Nicole's name and ours will be pristine. No scandal. No moving towns. I'll get you hired back on at the hospital." I brush my hands together. "We go on with our lives."

Ruby's gaze shifts back and forth across my face like she's

trying to figure out if I'm serious. When I don't look away, she swallows hard. "Seems like that's the only way," she whispers.

I shrug. "There's the other way, but that would harm innocent people. This plan would bring justice and also keep from harming you and me."

Ruby blows out a breath and then takes another sip of water. I notice her hand is shaking as she holds the glass. "Okay. I think it's decided, then."

"We need to plan where and how. We have to make sure it's deemed a suicide."

"We need her to write a note. Her own handwriting, explaining that she's doing poorly. Can't strap you down in marriage and make you miserable. Something like that."

I nod. Suicide notes always speak volumes. "I'll see if I can get her to write it. I might have to give her something to make her confused. Then we'll have to wait for the drugs I've been giving her to leave her system."

Ruby puts her hand on mine. "How do we do it? And who? You or me?"

Her question knocks the wind from my lungs. It's one thing to plot to kill your fiancée. It's another to actually follow through with the fatal blow. I flip my hand over and slide my fingers through Ruby's, squeezing hard. We're going to need to lean on each other to get this done. In fact, she and I will be inexplicably linked for the rest of our lives. Both of us will be keeping a horrible secret. Both of us will have stopped a killer.

My throat tightens up as I think of the different ways to actually kill Nicole and have it look like a suicide. Mental images are conjured up in my brain that cause me to start weeping.

Ruby pulls me into her arms and holds me, rocking side to side while I let it out. How did I get here? How did I go from my wedding day to planning my fiancée's murder? Everything I hoped for in my future has gone up in smoke. All because of what? Nicole's sudden bloodthirst? A side effect of a drug that never would have been in her system if she didn't have to have an organ transplant?

"Shh," Ruby whispers, her hand stroking the back of my head. "I'll do it, okay?"

I try to get ahold of myself but the lack of sleep and the adrenaline dump have left me rocked emotionally. I nod into Ruby's shoulder, relieved and a little ashamed that she's going to be the one to do it.

"Do you trust me, Asher?" Ruby asks a bit later as my tears finally abate.

I lift my head, letting her see my red-rimmed eyes and wet cheeks. I'm so far from the confident chief of medicine, I'm not even sure who that guy used to be. But Ruby doesn't look at me with disgust. She holds me by the arms with a look of understanding.

"I do trust you," I manage to say.

She nods as if it's all been decided. "Tomorrow, then. I'll take care of everything tomorrow."

And then she leaves, crawling into my bed and sleeping.

I do my part, feeding Nicole and then injecting her with a drug that I know causes her to be out of it. When her eyes are at half mast, I unknot the bands around her wrists and rub some feeling back into her arms. I place a TV tray on her lap and prop pillows behind her back. A sheet of paper and a pen are laid out next.

"Wha' you doin'?" she slurs, taking the pen and letting me fold her fingers around it.

I brush her hair back from her face and try to remember how I felt when I first met her at the hospital. She was so lovely. Innocent. The kind of nurse who was whip smart and still naive enough to think she could change the face of medicine by sheer will. I loved that about her. She cared about her patients. It wasn't about the paycheck like so many others. How could Nicole have gone from that girl to the woman who sits before me, admitting to killing innocent people?

"I love you, darling," I whisper one last time, throat closing on the last word. Her eyebrows dance higher on her forehead.

"Love you, too," she slurs back. Her eyes are bloodshot, but still that soft blue I used to love so much.

Part of me wants to be fanciful like Ruby and think Nicole is still somehow in there. But I saw what she did on that camera inside Ella's house. I saw the flights and gas receipts. I know what she's capable of. She has to be stopped.

"I want you to write about your nightmares, Nicole. Explain how they've been driving you insane. How you can't sleep. Can't eat. Can't possibly marry me with all this going on. How you don't know if you want to even keep living."

"Write it?" Her head slips to the side, and I worry I gave her too much of the drug. I hold her head straight and look her in the eyes.

"Write it all down. Like a diary."

I put her hand on the paper, position the pen, and let go, stepping back to sit in the chair in the corner. Nicole drops the pen but picks it back up and begins to write. I'm not sure if it will be legible or if it will make sense. I hope to God she doesn't write that she murdered people. Frame it all as nightmares and we should be fine. Anyone will be able to see she was out of her right mind.

I wait until her hand slips off the page and she slumps over. She's passed out. I shift closer and read what she wrote. It's harrowing. Dark and disturbed dreams. Paranoia. The panic and confusion she's been dealing with for months is painfully obvious.

And it's perfect for a suicide note.

uby

I'M LIVING IN A NIGHTMARE.

Yesterday, I was supposed to be a bridesmaid in my best friend's wedding. Instead, I spent the day plotting her murder.

Asher's pretty sure I have a concussion, but there's no time to rest. Every time I try to sleep, I end up having nightmares that wake me up, only to find out my reality is just as bad as the nightmares. I promised him I'd take care of Nicole today.

And yes, that's the way I'm framing it in my head. I'm going to *take care* of her. She's clearly mentally insane. She's got bags under her eyes. She's lost weight to the point of looking sickly. She's killed multiple people and then blacked it all out. She tried to kill *me*! I have the scab across my throat to prove it. Asher and I have no choice but to bring justice for what she's done.

Killing her and making it look like a suicide is a mercy.

She won't be in jail for the rest of her life, nor will her name be dragged through the mud as a nurse turned serial killer. Knowing Josephine, she'll start a fundraiser for mental health and prop Nicole up as some sort of saint just to keep the Kingsley name sparkling.

Rolling out of Asher's bed, I stretch and pull on clean jeans and a T-shirt. He drove me to my duplex last night to get everything I need for today. He also insisted I stay at his house in case anything happened overnight with Nicole. I think he didn't want to be alone in that big house with her any longer. I don't blame him.

Once dressed, I leave the bedroom to find Asher. He said he'd sleep on the couch, but when I get to the living room, he's nowhere to be found. The couch doesn't even have a blanket on it.

"Asher?"

"In here," he calls back.

I head in the direction his voice came from, finding him in the kitchen, sipping a cup of coffee and staring out the window.

"Sleep okay?" I ask. It's a dumb question. Of course he didn't sleep well. I have a feeling neither of us will sleep well ever again.

He grunts and I take that as a no. I walk behind him and fill up my own coffee cup. I'm going to need all the caffeine possible on board to do what I have to do today. I find flavored creamer in the refrigerator and pour that in.

"Our neighbors don't have Charlie anymore," Asher says quietly, still staring out the window.

I follow his line of vision, seeing the backyard of their neighbor's place where their German shepherd used to run free. "Maybe he died of old age?"

Asher shakes his head, still sipping his coffee. "No, he was only five."

I shrug. Honestly, I have bigger things to focus on today. "Have you checked on her this morning?"

"Yeah. She's awake. I fed her some yogurt and tried to talk to her. She didn't make much sense. I got a note out of her last night though. Should work." He tilts his head toward the kitchen island where a piece of paper sits all by itself.

I lean in closer and read it, grimacing the further I get. It's disturbing and quite convincing that Nicole is not well. Putting my coffee down, I fold my arms across my chest and spell out my plan to Asher. If he has concerns, now is the time to say something.

"I'm going to take her to your parents' cabin. I figure a suicide where her wedding was supposed to be will make a lot of sense. Are you okay with that? Do they have a security system? Anyone who visits on occasion that I need to be aware of?"

Asher blows out a long breath and puts his coffee cup in the sink. His head is bowed, the bent line of his spine spelling out defeat. I've never seen him this way, but finding out your fiancée is a murderer would do it.

"Yeah. That's a good plan. No one is out there. No cameras, no neighbors for miles."

He lifts his head and finally makes eye contact. I wish he wouldn't have. His eyes are haunted and red rimmed. He looks awful.

"How?" he asks simply.

This is the most bizarre conversation I've ever had. My heart aches just thinking about what I have to do. The only thing getting me through is knowing the woman I loved, the woman who instantly became my best friend years ago is already gone. She's buried so deep she'll never find her way out again. The old Nicole would want me to put her out of her misery. I know that deep in my soul.

"She has abrasions on her wrists, so I'll have a knife there that she'll have tried to use on her wrists. When that doesn't work, she'll swallow a whole handful of her pain meds. An overdose seems like the most humane way."

Asher looks crushed. His head drops and his breath is unsteady. Long minutes tick by while I wait him out. I won't do anything unless we're both in agreement. This only works if he and I are on the same page the whole way.

His jaw is solid as granite when he finally lifts his head. "Do it."

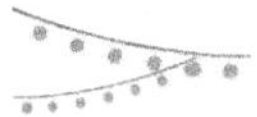

THE RIDE OUT to the cabin is uneventful. Asher helped me place Nicole in the back seat of her car. She's still restrained at the wrist and ankles, but we cleaned her up best we could and put her in a clean outfit. She's still out of it with some of the leftover pain pills we gave her from after her surgery. Asher swears any drugs he used on her the last two days have dissipated now, leaving only the drugs she was prescribed by legit doctors in her blood stream.

The switchbacks that lead to the remote cabin force me to drive slowly and carefully. I've been out here a few times over the years and I know the turnoff to the cabin is almost hidden, unless you know where to look. Normally, Asher or Nicole would be driving, so I'm having to pay even closer attention so I don't drive right by it.

Aha! There's the mailbox with the yellow numbers. I slow, put on my blinker even though I haven't seen any other traffic for miles and miles, and turn onto the road. The car bumps along potholes for a few hundred feet until we get to the smoothly paved area that leads to the cabin.

Calling it a cabin seems a bit ridiculous. You could fit two of my duplexes into the square footage of this upscale mansion in the woods. I park out front and get out, inhaling lungfuls of fresh pine-scented air. Trees surround the cabin so thickly it feels like the only house in existence. Not a sound makes it to my ears except for the rustle of wind in the branches and the scuttle of animals in the forest.

It's so peaceful here.

Except for what I have to do.

Nicole starts mumbling in the back of the car, though she doesn't make any sense. Pulling gloves from my pocket, I slip them on, already going through a mental checklist of what I need to do to execute this perfectly. My and Asher's future depends on it. I leave Nicole in the car for now and go unlock the cabin.

The heavy scent of roses hits my nose first. I gasp, taking in the line of bouquets lying on the dining table. They look stunning with their deep red petals, green leaves, and fresh baby's breath all wrapped up in perfect white ribbon. I let out something that sounds like a sob in the quiet of the forest.

Those would have been the bouquets for her wedding yesterday.

Left here to die.

Just like Nicole will be soon.

Asher should have warned me they'd be here. I swipe a hand across my cheeks to dry my tears and force myself to look away. I can grieve later, but today, I have a job to do.

Nicole's purse gets dumped on the kitchen counter, the contents strewn across the surface like a woman who's hit rock bottom. The bottle of pain pills goes back in my pocket for future use. Her knife is placed on the coffee table.

I push over a chair and unfold one of the throw blankets

on the back of the couch to drop it on the floor. This place needs to look like a distraught woman spent her last minutes here wrestling her mental health in the wake of a canceled wedding. When I have everything ready, I take another steadying breath, ignore the cloying rose scent that's nearly choking me, and head back outside to get Nicole.

Except when I get there, the back door is open and Asher is lifting her out and holding her to his chest.

"Asher! What are you doing?" I fly down the three porch steps and race toward him. His truck is parked behind Nicole's car, blocking me in. This was not a part of the plan.

He looks at me with regret. "I had to be here."

Before I can reply, he starts walking into the cabin, Nicole in his arms, her head flopped against his chest and the duct tape around her wrists and ankles gone. I trail after them, feeling a little alarmed at this last-minute change. He sits on the couch and settles Nicole in his arms. She blinks her eyes open, partially aware of what's going on thanks to the drugs leaving her system for the two hours it took to drive up here.

"I thought you were going to go into the hospital so you had an alibi?"

Asher doesn't answer nor look at me. He just holds Nicole while the two stare at each other. My heart starts pounding. Has he changed his mind?

"Let me go," Nicole pleas, her fingers sliding along his jaw where his beard has grown out far past his occasional five o'clock shadow.

Asher gulps back tears. "I can't, darling. You've done too much."

Nicole shakes her head slowly. "But...it's your fault!"
Asher frowns.

"It is!" she insists. Her fingers drop from his chin to grip his shirt. "You put me on the top of that transplant list! You're the reason I got that murderer's heart!"

Asher shakes his head. "No. I swear to you I didn't do that."

"You did!" Nicole screams, her voice fading away into sobs. She feebly punches his chest and drops her face to his shoulder. "You did."

Asher looks at me, his jaw tight. "Give her the pills."

# CHAPTER TWENTY-SIX

sher

IN THE END, Nicole went in peace.

Or at least, in as much peace as she could under the circumstances.

Lying there in my arms, sobbing, Nicole began to still long minutes later. She lifted her head to gaze up at me, eyelids swollen, snot and tears mixing all over her face. Her bottom lip trembled. But it was her eyes that did me in. For just a brief moment, it was like looking into the eyes of the woman I'd fallen in love with. Everything dark and sinister cleared from them. The blue pulsed brighter, I would swear it.

"I'm sorry," she whispered, the sides of her mouth turned down. "I love you." She swiveled her head and locked eyes with Ruby. "I love you too and I'm sorry."

Then she let go of my shirt and held out her hand, palm up, fingers cupped. "Give me the pills."

Ruby, with her own tears streaming down her face, opened

the orange pill container and dumped the pills into Nicole's hand. Nicole threw them in her mouth all at once, no hesitation washing them down with the water bottle Ruby provided her.

The three of us sat there in stunned, heartbreaking silence. No words could possibly make this right. My arms trembled as I held Nicole, knowing it would be for the last time. Very quickly her head bobbed to the side and her eyes became unfocused.

She looked up at me one last time, licked her lips, and spoke. "It ends here."

Then she closed her eyes, laid her head on my shoulder, and peacefully slipped into eternal rest. I held her long after her chest quit rising and falling. Ruby sat across from us, the occasional sob or hitched inhale echoing in the empty cabin.

When the sun set and the cabin became bathed in darkness, I leaned down and kissed Nicole's forehead for the last time. It was almost poetic for her last inhale to be infused with the scent of roses. My beautiful girl loved her red roses.

I felt numb to the pain. I felt like life would never be joyful again. This secret would be lodged in my heart forever, anchoring me down in a depression that would never lift. I stood up, only to gently lean back down and arrange Nicole on the couch. Ruby also stood, pulling another throw blanket from the back of the couch and covered Nicole's lap. My arms already felt empty.

It was Ruby who ultimately got me out of that cabin when my feet didn't seem capable of leaving. She arranged the scene to look exactly like what it was: a suicide. A desperately lost, guilt-ridden woman who needed an escape from what her life had become. Ruby made sure all the details were in place, then she physically pulled me from the cabin and locked it up. We stood by Nicole's car, both of us exhausted and emotionally spent.

"Can you drive?"

I blink and focus on my friend. "Yeah, I think so."

"Let's go back to your house." She bites her bottom lip and looks around at the trees we can barely make out in the darkness. "I don't want to be alone. Is that okay?"

I nod, latching on to her idea. I don't want to be alone either. The loneliness and heartbreak will rush in soon enough. I need just one more night where I don't have to face everything that has happened on my own.

"Get in the car. I'll drive," I say simply, turning on my heel and leaving the cabin for good. Ruby climbs into the passenger seat of my truck. I can't even look at the cabin as we back down the driveway and the headlights illuminate the place.

After Nicole's body is discovered by the cleaners who come once a week, I'll beg my parents to sell the place. I know for sure I can never step foot on this property again. I'll rip up every rose bush on our property back in Rosebud Grove just so I don't have to smell their sweet perfume and be reminded of the wedding that never happened and the woman whose face used to light up at the sight of them.

We make it back to my house two hours later in the dark. I click the garage door opener and nearly choke when I see the empty space where Nicole's car is supposed to be. I should let Ruby move her clunker inside the garage overnight, but I can't replace Nicole, not even just a parking spot.

We step inside the house, the clank of my keys hitting the kitchen island echoing in the emptiness. Ruby spins in a circle. When she finally looks in my direction, we both just stare at each other. Lost. Broken.

"What do we do?" Ruby whispers.

I swallow hard and try to think. My brain feels as fuzzy as Nicole's probably was there at the end. God. The end. My fiancée is dead. My hand rubs my sternum but there's nothing that'll take away the ache.

"We need to shower. Make sure we have no evidence on us. We'll clean up the guest room. I'll take the truck to get it washed tomorrow in case there's mud on the tires or something." Logic is something I can cling to.

Ruby nods, looking as devastated as I feel. "I'll take the guest shower." She points her thumb over her shoulder, then turns and walks in that direction. I head for the primary bedroom, my heart breaking as I take in the space where Nicole and I were to start a family. To be husband and wife. To begin our lives together.

I rush through to the bathroom and realize my towel is in the dirty clothes hamper. Reaching under the sink, I pull out a clean towel and knock something over. Probably one of Nicole's many bottles of lotion, conditioner, or shampoo. The woman never saw a beauty product she didn't want to try.

Except, as I pick up the box, I realize it's none of those things.

It's a pregnancy test.

Already opened and used.

A *positive* pregnancy test.

An inhumane wail bounces off the walls and it takes me a solid minute to realize it's me. I've somehow slid down the wall, my knees curled up into my chest as I cradle the pregnancy test in my hands. Sobs and gut-wrenching wails erupt from my throat as I try to process so much pain. It's too much. Far too much for one person to bear.

Ruby finds me there, wet hair dripping onto her pajamas. Her gaze quickly takes in the scene and her face crumples. She drops to the floor, leans her back against the wall next to me, and wraps her arms around my shoulders.

The dam breaks. I fall into her, my tears adding to the wetness of her pajamas. I let her comfort me as one would a doting mother. I feel no older than a toddler, overwhelmed with big emotions I don't know what to do with. How can someone process something so horrible? Something so unfair. I truly believe I'd break into a thousand pieces if she wasn't right there holding me together.

Time has no meaning in the place I've descended to. I'm not sure if it's the middle of the night when Ruby lifts me off the floor and forces me onto the bed. My tears have dried up and I've entered some sort of catatonic phase where nothing matters any longer. Ruby throws a blanket over me and then curls up behind me, her arm around my waist. I grab her hand and hold it to my chest, desperate to know I'm not alone.

And that's how I fall asleep, the day after what was supposed to be my wedding day. My fiancée is dead and another woman is in my bed.

I had no idea life could be this cruel.

No idea that the sins of another could ruin my life just by proximity.

# CHAPTER TWENTY-SEVEN

*J*osephine

"I'm sorry it had to end this way."

I turn my head to see Gerald Weathersfield stepping to my side, his black suit coat barely containing his extended gut. It's disgusting how little he cares for his health, but his deep pockets are quite lovely. He and I have been on several boards together, and I'm grateful I was smart enough to make him my ally years ago. One of those *keep your enemies closer* sort of scenarios.

I gaze out at the sea of people gathered at the cemetery this morning, all dressed in somber tones. The tall pines that surround this plot have cast the group in shadows. Quite a few mourners have availed themselves of the tissues strategically placed at the end of each row of chairs. It never ceases to amaze me how many people cared for Nicole Kelly.

Her father, of course, has been inconsolable since he

arrived in town the day after our cleaning staff found Nicole's body at our summer cabin just days after their canceled wedding. The poor man blames himself for her suicide, claiming he knew she was troubled when she visited him, but he brushed it off as wedding jitters. Quite frankly, his blubbering and constant reminiscing about Nicole are starting to wear on me.

My beloved son is also a shell of his normal self. I haven't seen his beautiful smile in weeks. I still can't understand what he saw in that girl. Nicole came from a poor town in New Mexico, a lowly nurse with a painfully average intelligence. Add in the faulty heart and why the hell Asher would seek to chain himself to her was beyond me.

I lift a shoulder and let it fall. Memories of her grabbing my wrist at the gala and threatening me push back any guilt I may feel for my own part in her demise. The woman was unstable.

"No, you're not and neither am I. But my son will move on. Find love somewhere else." I turn back to Gerald, doing my best to hold back a grin. "And we'll find other patients to test."

Gerald frowns, his cheeks pressing impossibly wide as he purses his lips. "This experiment was wildly successful. If we can replicate it, we can get a grant to do another experiment."

"Above board this time, of course," I add.

Gerald nods, blinking his beady eyes. "We have to be careful picking our next bunch. They must be spread out more geographically."

"Agreed." That's what I like about Gerald. All business. All about profit. And he's not afraid to engage in some shady dealings if it means a good outcome at the end.

People start migrating to their cars, the inevitable end of the public funeral. Rosebud Grove's golden girl is gone. It's chilly out, though we were blessed not to have rain. I see my husband talking to some woman I don't know. He's got his hand on her arm. I roll my eyes and decide to break things up. I can't deal with another affair of his right now. Not when I'm still dealing with Asher. These men in my life are so damn needy.

"Let's set up a call later this week to discuss the next round."

Gerald nods, compressing his three chins. "I'll go shake hands and find new donors."

Not even a funeral stops that man.

I leave him and insert myself into my husband's conversation. The woman, her lips and tits plumped up so much she looks comical, quickly excuses herself. Smart woman. Far too smart for my husband. My grip on my husband's arm is bruising as we turn to console Asher. My sweet boy hugs the last mourner, accepts their condolences, and sighs like he's got the weight of the world on his shoulders as they step away.

I slip my arm around his waist and pat his chest. He's lost weight and I don't like seeing that. He's taken Nicole's death hard, of course. They were set to be married.

But I know it's more than that.

My summer cabin has cameras, of course. What kind of woman owns multiple properties and doesn't keep an eye on them? Because I couldn't get ahold of Asher or Nicole when they canceled their wedding last minute, I took it upon myself to track my boy. For safety purposes I have a tracking device on his truck. I saw he was at the cabin and availed myself of the cameras from my phone. I both saw and heard everything that happened that day. I saw Ruby and Asher assist Nicole with taking her own life. Of course, I drove up there the next day to disconnect the cameras and destroy any evidence that may have cast a shadow on our good name.

I won't lie, I'm deeply proud of my son for following through on what he did. It takes character to end the life of someone you've loved. To confront the character flaws that are not compatible with society and certainly not with a happy marriage. He did the right thing. Full stop.

I'm also elated that Nicole is out of the picture finally. The idea of her joining our family used to keep me up at night. Make me nauseous just thinking about it.

All my plans have unfolded even better than I could have imagined two years ago when I set this whole thing in motion.

You see, Gerald approached me over two years ago with groundbreaking research being done in the field of organ transplant. One young scientist postured that cells outside of the brain retain memory. Of course, the cell doesn't retain vivid memories like our brains do, but the cell has an instinctive ability to remember. An instinct programmed in the cells that comes from the desires and deeds of the human it came from. We all know traumatic emotional events are stored in the tissues as physical trauma. Not hard to make the leap that personality, genius, and even morality are also stored on a cellular level.

Gerald saw dollar signs, of course. Could we prove this theory of cell memory and use it to procure donated organs from geniuses, which are then implanted into other people, thereby upcycling human intelligence? The smarter we become as a species, the richer we become too. Granted, the vast majority of lay people wouldn't have access to these organs. They'd come at a price. A steep one. And we'd be the ones to collect that price.

As with anything in science and business, it's the first person to the table with a novel idea that makes the lion's share of the money. So, we cut some corners and kept things quiet while we figured out exactly what we had here.

While I wanted to make money, I also had a problem to solve.

Nicole.

How could I get Asher to call off the wedding?

And that's when my genius idea came to me. Gerald was skeptical at first, thinking I was trying to prove his idea wrong. That wasn't the case. If we could prove cells from a morally bankrupt person could affect good people, the inverse could be proven as well. And who better to experiment on than prison inmates of the serial killer variety? No one looks in on their wellbeing, after all.

With his backing, I was able to reach out to the next scheduled death row inmate. Cyrus Gene Bixler in Texas. Sadly, most states don't carry out death sentences any longer, but you can always count on Texas in a pinch. Through layers of shell companies, Gerald was able to procure the rights to Mr. Bixler's organs and coordinate with the prison medical team. Gerald told me Mr. Bixler was all too happy to have his organs used after his death. Something about an eye for an eye.

Meanwhile, I broke into the national organ donation list and moved my sweet future daughter-in-law to the top of the list for a new heart the day before Mr. Bixler was executed. From there, Gerald and I watched it all unfold like dominoes laid out in an intricate design.

Not only did we definitely prove that evil can spread via cells that remember and yearn for violence, Nicole was taken care of for me. I followed all the recipients, observing from afar. They all began to lose their minds, have memories that weren't theirs, or in one case, develop a Texas twang they never had before. The shift in each of them was remarkable. Now Gerald and I can conduct another experiment, this one proving that genius can spread as well.

"Sir, we'd like to lower the casket, if you're ready."

The funeral home has coordinated with Asher and Nicole's father, the two men making her final arrangements like she was something precious. I've had to bite my tongue and will my eyes not to roll into the back of my head with all their plans to honor their golden girl. There was nothing golden about Nicole except for the dollar signs I saw in her eyes when they landed on my son.

Asher nods and moves away from me to stand next to Nicole's casket. Nicole's father openly weeps as they begin to lower her casket into the ground. He's giving me a headache with all that sobbing.

Ruby slides quietly up to Asher. My eyes narrow as I see Asher put his arm around her shoulders and pull her in close. Those two have gotten chummy over the last few weeks. I can't decide if there's a romance budding there or if they've just bonded over killing Nicole. The fact that they plan to take a trip to Hawaii together, using the hotel and flights he booked for his honeymoon has me on guard. He says it'll be good therapy for them after all they've gone through, but I wonder if there's more to it.

"Ashes to ashes," the minister begins.

I zone him out, his words offering me no comfort against the sudden buzz of nerves below my ribs. Only family has stayed behind for the burial, which somehow includes Ruby. Since when did *she* become family? I stare at her, the way her inappropriately showy curves are pressed against my son. Her gaze is on the casket and tears slip down her cheeks like you'd expect at a funeral. But it's the hand that stays on Asher's stomach that has me seeing red. Her index finger is sweeping up and down, up and down. As if she has any right to touch Asher so intimately. In such a "more than friends" way.

When the minister is done lying about how wonderful Nicole was, completely naive to the murders left in her wake, Asher throws the first clump of dirt onto the casket, followed by Nicole's father, and then Ruby. When it's my turn, I stare down at the wooden box Nicole will forever rest in. I don't say a prayer. I issue a promise instead. One she might actually agree with me on.

*If she's after Asher, I promise you I'll take care of her.*

# EPILOGUE

$S$ mall Town, Texas

"I UNDERSTAND this whole process comes with invasive procedures and endless blood draws, but today is one that most couples say is one of their favorites." The woman smiles at the couple, like they're all at a county fair discussing which ride to go on next and not at a fertility clinic where couples go when they can't get pregnant.

The room is a sterile light gray, every surface sanitized and devoid of any personality. The doctor prefers it that way, says it's soothing to patients. The woman thinks maybe the doctor is too cheap to spring for decor.

She dramatically snaps open the binder, running her long tipped-red nail down the page of headshots and descriptions. "We pride ourselves on having the widest variety of sperm donors. Every possible physical quality or background is represented here."

The couple stares down at the thick binder with excitement and just a bit of overwhelm. The wife's cheeks heat and she fumbles over her words. "Wow. This is a bit like online dating, huh?"

The husband's eyebrows furrow. "Online dating? No. You're married. This is just picking out the shiniest apple of the bunch."

The wife, chastised, looks at the woman. "Are there any...*bad apples* we should be aware of?"

The woman shows off her brilliantly white teeth. "Absolutely not. We've done thorough background checks and interviews before anyone makes it into this binder." Her nail stabs the page for emphasis.

"Okay, great," the wife mumbles back.

"I'll give you all the time you need to sort through them," the woman says, standing and excusing herself from the small conference room.

She quietly closes the door behind her and walks to the break room where a couple nurses are eating a snack in between procedures. They look up and one of them scoots a metal chair out for her to sit in. She sinks into the chair and loses the megawatt smile.

"What's wrong?" one nurse asks.

The woman sighs, the guilt weighing her down. Maybe if she tells someone, she'll feel better. She clasps her hands together on the table and decides to unload. They've been friends and coworkers for years. These two nurses work directly with Dr. Sutherland. Surely they'll know the truth and be able to put her mind at ease.

"Doc had me input a bunch of new names in the binder last week," she begins. "But when I asked him how the interviews had gone and what tests he runs on the candidates to make sure they're genetically healthy, he nearly bit my head off." The woman focuses on her hands, feeling a bit silly for where her imagination jumped to now that she's saying it out loud. "I've never seen men in here for the interviews. I just got the sense that there wasn't as much of a rigorous screening process as I thought."

The nurse who pushed out the chair reaches for her hands, hers cold and clammy. "You're being silly. Dr. Sutherland has the most rigorous screening process of any clinic we've worked at. Promise."

The woman looks at her, relieved to hear it. "Yeah?"

The nurse smiles and pats her hands.

They change the subject, chatting about their plans for the weekend. When the woman looks at her watch, she stands up, adjusts her dress, and makes her way back to the conference room. After a light tap on the door, she sticks her head inside. The couple swivels around to see who it is.

"How are we doing in here? Anything I can help with?"

The wife's cheeks are still flushed, but the husband looks exacerbated. "We're done."

"Great!" The woman steps inside, closes the door behind her, and resumes her seat behind the desk. "Who'd you choose?"

The man stabs his finger on a face. "This one is fine."

The woman swivels the binder around and looks at the man listed. "Oh, he looks like an excellent choice. Strong jaw, bright eyes, and an easy smile." She doesn't mention that the haircut seems a little old fashioned, like maybe the photo was taken a few decades ago. But that couldn't be right. Their candidates are always thoroughly vetted.

"He has such strong genes, don't you think?" the wife asks, clearly wanting reassurance. The woman give it to her, restating how thoroughly they screen their sperm donors. It's the spiel they taught her on her first day of work at this clinic.

The woman continues to smile at the couple, seeing excitement on the wife's face and impatience on the husband's. It's always this way. It makes sense. No man really enjoys picking out another man's sperm to impregnate his own wife because he can't get the job done himself. Male pride and all that.

She eventually nods, then swivels to her computer, marking down their choice in the patient's file. "Okay, since you've chosen insemination, it looks like we can get you in as quickly as your next ovulation period, which should be in ten days according to your menstruation history. Does that seem right?"

The wife nods and the husband checks his watch. A few more clicks on the computer and everything is set. The woman folds her hands together and smiles broadly at the couple.

"Okay. In ten days we'll see you back here. Our nurses will be in touch daily until then." She checks the binder. "C.G. Bixler's sample will be ready for you and we'll do everything in our power to get you pregnant on the first try. Thankfully, he gave us several samples, so we can try again if it doesn't take the first time."

The wife is overjoyed, tears welling up in her eyes. "Oh my God, this is really happening." She grabs her husband's hand. "We're finally going to have a baby!"

The End

## ABOUT THE AUTHOR

Gertie Greyson is an emerging author of domestic thrillers, with thirty books under her belt in other, less-scary genres. An empty nester with time on her hands and diabolical ideas in her head, Gertie lives in the South with her husband and newly acquired doodle puppy.

If you'd like to know more about Gertie or the other thriller novels she's currently writing, please join her newsletter here: https://www.subscribepage.com/gertieg

www.ingramcontent.com/pod-product-compliance
Lightning Source LLC
Chambersburg PA
CBHW070502200726
48293CB00007B/2335